Thoughts from Crudley, the cat:

I can't believe someone stole me, thinking I was Princess Athabasca. The kidnapper must certainly not be a cat lover if he mistook a tomcat like me for that pedigreed feline. My owner, Cass, must be frantic with worry. She's so sweet and loving, I know she would do anything to get me back home where I belong.

I'm hoping that the millionaire who's helping her with the search will sweep Cass off her feet and into his elegant mansion. Cass deserves to be happy, and Gabe Preston would be the luckiest man alive if he married her. Then all my catnip wishes and caviar dreams would finally come true. He'll put me in fancy collars and Cass in beautiful jewels...maybe they'll even have a few babies who'll play with me!

I'll just have to keep my paws crossed and wait to see what happens....

Dear Reader,

Silhouette welcomes popular author Judy Christenberry to the Romance line with a touching story that will enchant readers in every age group. In *The Nine-Month Bride*, a wealthy rancher who wants an heir and a prim librarian who wants a baby marry for convenience, but imminent parenthood makes them rethink their vows....

Next, Moyra Tarling delivers the emotionally riveting BUNDLES OF JOY tale of a mother-to-be who discovers that her child's father doesn't remember his own name— let alone the night they'd created their *Wedding Day Baby*. Karen Rose Smith's miniseries DO YOU TAKE THIS STRANGER? continues with *Love, Honor and a Pregnant Bride*, in which a jaded cowboy learns an unexpected lesson in love from an expectant beauty.

Part of our MEN! promotion, *Cowboy Dad* by Robin Nicholas features a deliciously handsome, duty-minded father aiming to win the heart of a woman who's sworn off cowboys. Award-winning Marie Ferrarella launches her latest miniseries, LIKE MOTHER, LIKE DAUGHTER, with *One Plus One Makes Marriage*. Though the math sounds easy, the road to "I do" takes some emotional twists and turns for this feisty heroine and the embittered man she loves. And Romance proudly introduces Patricia Seeley, one of Silhouette's WOMEN TO WATCH. A ransom note—for a cat!—sets the stage where *The Millionaire Meets His Match*.

Hope you enjoy this month's offerings!

Mary-Theresa Hussey
Senior Editor, Silhouette Romance

Please address questions and book requests to:
Silhouette Reader Service
U.S.: 3010 Walden Ave., P.O. Box 1325, Buffalo, NY 14269
Canadian: P.O. Box 609, Fort Erie, Ont. L2A 5X3

THE MILLIONAIRE MEETS HIS MATCH

Patricia Seeley

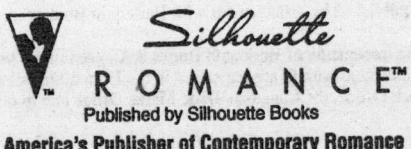

Published by Silhouette Books
America's Publisher of Contemporary Romance

If you purchased this book without a cover you should be aware that this book is stolen property. It was reported as "unsold and destroyed" to the publisher, and neither the author nor the publisher has received any payment for this "stripped book."

For "Daddycakes"

 SILHOUETTE BOOKS

ISBN 0-373-19329-7

THE MILLIONAIRE MEETS HIS MATCH

Copyright © 1998 by Patricia Seeley

All rights reserved. Except for use in any review, the reproduction or utilization of this work in whole or in part in any form by any electronic, mechanical or other means, now known or hereafter invented, including xerography, photocopying and recording, or in any information storage or retrieval system, is forbidden without the written permission of the editorial office, Silhouette Books, 300 East 42nd Street, New York, NY 10017 U.S.A.

All characters in this book have no existence outside the imagination of the author and have no relation whatsoever to anyone bearing the same name or names. They are not even distantly inspired by any individual known or unknown to the author, and all incidents are pure invention.

This edition published by arrangement with Harlequin Books S.A.

® and TM are trademarks of Harlequin Books S.A., used under license. Trademarks indicated with ® are registered in the United States Patent and Trademark Office, the Canadian Trade Marks Office and in other countries.

Printed in U.S.A.

PATRICIA SEELEY

graduated from the University of Denver with a degree in English. She has worked as a bakery clerk, a secretarial assistant, a waitress and a police dispatcher, and has even classified and identified fingerprints. She currently works in the adjustments division of a bank, searching various documents and computer data for missing money.

She grew up on the East Coast but came to Oregon to dog-and-cat-and-house-sit for a friend who was going on a walking tour of Europe for six months. By the time her friend had returned, Patricia had developed an attachment to the beautiful state, in spite of all the rain.

Patricia and her husband of ten years have one cat, who was semi-namelessly referred to as "The Kitty" for the first eight years they had her, and who is now technically named Kitty Sue.

The Silhouette Spotlight
"Where Passion Lives"

MEET WOMAN TO WATCH *Patricia Seeley*

What was your inspiration for THE MILLIONAIRE MEETS HIS MATCH?

PS: I saw two unrelated articles concerning missing pets that became the basis for the plot. Using the idea of a cat kidnapping as the impetus for bringing the hero and heroine together, I thought about the various roles each might play that would bring them together and at the same time create a conflict between them.

What about the Silhouette Romance line appeals to you as a reader and as a writer?

PS: I like the old-fashioned, sweet and innocently sexy feeling of the Romance line. I'm a fan of old 1940s films, particularly Claudette Colbert movies. I love the tone of those movies—romantic attraction played out with warmth, humor and clear but understated sexiness.

Why is THE MILLIONAIRE MEETS HIS MATCH special to you?

PS: I really like the characters in this book. The narrative line is so strongly character driven that it was always easy to pick up where I had left off. I also like the humor. And I really did have a cat named Crudley, and it was fun to use him in the story.

Chapter One

"What do you mean he's gone?" Cass Appleton glared across the wide expanse of teak desk at the office manager safely shielded behind it.

Mr. Howard, as his brass nameplate proclaimed him, smiled with a practiced artificial concern that said he was used to dealing with overwrought women. "Simply that," he said in his most consciously soothing voice. "When the attendants arrived this morning, they found the door open..."

"I don't believe it!" Cass slapped both hands on the polished wood surface of the desk. "How could you let this happen? I told you he could slip off those ridiculous hook latches you use on the doors. I told you that you'd need to take extra precautions. It's sheer negligence for you to have let him escape despite my warnings. With the rates you charge, the least I have a right to expect is that you won't—" She broke off, unwilling to admit the harsh reality. "Won't...misplace my cat. Have you checked behind all the furniture?"

"My dear Miss Appleton, you didn't allow me to finish. It wasn't simply your cat's cage that was found open, but the rear door of the clinic itself. We were burglarized last night."

Cass continued to stare at him, unappeased. "Are you trying to tell me someone broke in here and stole my cat?"

Surprise ruffled briefly across Mr. Howard's carefully composed features before he regained his self-possession. "Of course not," he assured her. "Your animal, as you know, has very little monetary value. I meant that although your cat did, apparently, manage to get out of his cage, he still would have been perfectly safe and sound inside the clinic building had we not experienced this unforeseeable break-in. I'm happy to say our alarm system worked perfectly and the thieves were frightened off before any of the expensive drugs or equipment could be taken. Unfortunately, your—" he dropped his gaze to the file folder on his desk "—Cuddly evidently used the opportunity to run off through the outer office doors."

"*Crud*-ley," Cass corrected him through gritted teeth.

"Pardon?" Mr. Howard asked as if suspecting he'd just been sworn at in some foreign tongue.

"His name is Crudley, not Cuddly. The *r* isn't silent."

Mr. Howard straightened his tie and relaxed fractionally. "Oh. Of course. In any case, I did send the boys out immediately to search the area as soon as I was informed one of the animals was missing. But on these busy streets, with all the early-morning traffic that rushes by, they weren't able to find any sign of him." He shrugged philosophically, apparently able to detach himself from the unpleasant reality of the fate he'd just suggested Cass's cat would inevitably meet.

"All I can do now," he continued, "is tender the doctor's sincere sympathy for your loss and my personal apologies for the negligence of the kennel staff. I assure you, they will be sharply reprimanded for this oversight. Naturally you won't be charged for your cat's two days' board. And although there is no question of your suffering any financial loss by your cat's disappearance, the doctor has instructed me to offer you a free replacement, with all its shots, and a free neutering when the time comes. We have several nice kittens available right now, if you'd care to pick one out. Then we can all put this unpleasant incident behind us."

Cass felt the hot color rising to her cheeks. "I don't want a 'replacement.' I want Crudley back. I left him in your care. You're responsible. Do something." The last words came out almost a plea, and Cass instantly despised herself for asking anything of this heartless petty functionary. Were there people who could be appeased by the kind of cold-blooded drivel Mr. Howard had been spouting? Or was she merely too inconsequential to rate a conference with the clinic's owner himself? "I want to talk to Dr. Bellingham," she declared.

The office manager shook his head and sighed. "I'm afraid that will be impossible. The doctor's schedule is quite full for the next several days—the annual dog show, you know. In any case, I assure you I have followed precisely the doctor's instructions on this matter. There is nothing further that he, or I, can do for you."

Cass stood and smoothed the creases from her rapidly wilting summer suit. "We'll see about that," she said, hoping but doubting that the words sounded vaguely ominous.

The office manager smirked priggishly and barely inclined his head in acknowledgment of her empty threat, then rose fluidly to open the door for her to leave.

Outside, the late-afternoon sun still blazed high in the sky, sending waves of heat rippling up from the hot asphalt parking lot. The scorching air suddenly seemed too suffocating to inhale, and Cass staggered slightly as she tried to catch her breath.

She never should have brought Crudley to this callous overpriced clinic. She'd deliberately chosen the most expensive veterinarian in town, a man whose patrons included most of the elite in Newport society, believing Crudley would receive the best possible care from him. Now, it turned out, she had been wrong to assume he was well cared for.

Cass stalked over to her car, threw open the door and then slammed it shut behind her. Shoving the key in the ignition, she started the engine with an unnecessary roar and turned the air-conditioning on full. The cooling blast did little to ease the fevered anguish that overwhelmed her. It was too much. On top of everything else that had been miserable and hopeless in the past three days, now Crudley was gone.

Gone. The word brought such a spasm of pain to her midsection that Cass felt nauseated, such a tightening of her throat that she could scarcely breathe. She slumped over the steering wheel and rested her head on her forearms, feeling the tears well up in her eyes and overflow down her flushed cheeks.

A gentle tapping on her window startled her. Cass looked up to see Bobby, one of the kennel attendants, peering anxiously at her through the glass. She pushed the air-conditioning switch to a lower setting and rolled down her window.

"Are you all right, Miss Appleton?" the boy asked. His brown eyes were warm with concern. Unlike most teenage boys, he didn't seem to be uneasy in the presence of someone else's emotional display.

Cass grabbed a tissue and quickly blotted her eyes. "I'm fine, Bobby. Thanks. I just had some bad news."

Bobby glanced around the parking lot furtively, then hunkered down beside her car, out of sight of anyone looking their way from the clinic. "I know," he said. "That's why I was waiting for you. I'm the one who opened up this morning and found Crudley gone." He shot a quick look in the direction of the building, then turned back to Cass. "He's a great cat, Miss Appleton. Not like most of them that come to this place, all pampered and spoiled with no personality. Crudley is a real character. And smart? Miss Appleton, I've never seen a smarter cat. You could teach him to do anything, I swear. Whenever I see him here, I make it a point to look after him myself and make sure all his instructions are followed to the letter. I would never let anything happen to him."

Cass experienced a rush of compassion for the boy. Unlike the office manager's prepared bromides and rehearsed apology, Bobby's words had the ring of truth. His feelings for her plight were genuine, based on his own affection for her cat. "It's not your fault," she assured him.

Bobby's eyes widened in surprise. "Oh, I know it's not. That's what I had to tell you. I've known Crudley for three years and I know he can pick locks and open doors on regular cages. I've seen him do it. During the day, if I'm working alone in the kennels, I let Crudley wander around with me while I feed the other animals and stuff. Then I play with him awhile before I put him away for the night. But before I leave, I always put a special lock on his door so he can't get loose during the night. I wouldn't want him to get hurt or anything."

Bobby gave the clinic another surreptitious glance. "Miss Appleton, Crudley was locked in tight last night. I saw to that. And then this morning, when I got here, he was gone, and someone had left a note for Dr. Bellingham. I heard the doctor and Mr. Howard talking about it, and then I sneaked into the office after they left and looked for it. It's just like the kind of ransom note you see in the movies."

"Ransom!" Cass interjected.

Bobby nodded. "Yes, ma'am. With words and letters cut out from old magazines and newspapers. It said that the kidnappers had taken Princess Athabasca and would be calling Mrs. Crosswhite tonight with instructions on how to get her cat back."

"Princess Athabasca?" Cass frowned. "Mrs. Crosswhite? There's another cat missing?"

"No, ma'am." Bobby shook his head emphatically. "Just Crudley. But the kidnappers think *he's* Princess Athabasca."

Cass pressed her fingers to her throbbing temples. "Bobby, I don't understand."

"That's because you haven't seen Princess Athabasca. She's a big gray cat with golden eyes." He paused, as if waiting to see if Cass had caught on. "Her breed is very rare and expensive, and she's a national champion, but she looks a lot like Crudley, even though he's just a regular cat. I would never get the two of them confused," Bobby assured Cass, "but someone who'd only seen a picture of the Princess or read a description and knew she would be here this weekend might make that mistake."

Cass at last began to understand the significance of what Bobby was explaining to her. "So someone *did* steal my cat," she summed up incredulously, "because they thought he was someone else's cat."

"Mrs. Crosswhite's," Bobby repeated. "She's filthy rich and crazy about her cat. The kidnappers are going to demand a ransom. Only they haven't got Princess Athabasca, and Mrs. Crosswhite's not going to know what they're talking about when they call."

Cass drew a sharp breath, remembering her own conversation with the office manager. "You mean Mr. Howard and Dr. Bellingham didn't tell Mrs. Crosswhite someone had tried to steal her cat?"

Bobby shook his head. "No, ma'am. They don't want anyone to know about it. They don't want the rich customers thinking their animals aren't safe here. They even told the police there was no need to make a report since nothing was taken. The chauffeur picked up Princess Athabasca this afternoon and took her home. When the kidnappers contact Mrs. Crosswhite tonight, she'll just think it's some prank and ignore it." Bobby's voice dropped to a whisper. "Then I don't know what will happen to Crudley."

Cass shared his unspoken fears, even as her heart leaped with the knowledge that, for the moment at least, Crudley was alive and safe. "Nothing is going to happen to him," she said firmly, patting Bobby's shoulder to reassure him. She turned and looked at the blankly imposing facade of the veterinary clinic. "I'm going back in there and force that weasel Mr. Howard to call Mrs. Crosswhite and tell her what's going on. Then I'm going to contact the police and have them put a trace on her phone so when the kidnappers call, we can find out who and where they are." In the space of a few seconds Cass had almost convinced herself that Crudley was on his way home already.

One look at Bobby's expression reminded Cass her problems were far from over just because she knew the reason for Crudley's disappearance. "I don't know," he said doubtfully. "I don't think anyone in there is going to help you." He made a grim face. "The old man isn't interested in anything but the bottom line, and he mostly hires people who can't afford to be anything but loyal. He doesn't want any scandal or bad publicity, and he'll lie if he has to. The official story by eight o'clock this morning was that someone tried to break in but was scared off by the alarms and never got inside. They've either hidden the kidnappers' note or destroyed it, because when I sneaked back into the office during lunch to look for it, it was gone. There's no way I can prove what I've told you, except for this."

Bobby pulled a padlock out of his pocket and handed it to Cass. "It's the one I used to lock Crudley in. Unless somebody slipped him a set of lock picks, Crudley didn't let himself out of that cage. Someone used the key I left on the board."

Cass stared at the lock. It was all the proof she needed. "I can't let them get away with this," she insisted. "And I have to do something to save Crudley."

"I know. Me, too. I've been thinking about it all day, trying to figure out what to do, and I decided we should go to Mrs. Crosswhite ourselves."

"Go ourselves?" Cass echoed, still trying to formulate a plan of action despite the tumult of emotions swirling in her head.

"Yes, ma'am. I figure if we tell her the story, she'll want to help. She's really a nice lady," Bobby said with the confidence of youth. "I've met her when she brings Princess in. She's a little dizzy, if you know what I mean, but good-hearted. She always pets the other animals and talks to them. She's pretty cool."

Bobby's idea wasn't half-bad. It was simple and direct, and it didn't rely on the dubious support of Dr. Bellingham or Mr. Howard. Cass's mind raced ahead. She would contact Mrs. Crosswhite, explain the situation, ask her to stall the kidnappers and then go to the police for their assistance. "It's a good plan," she told the young kennel attendant, "except for one thing. I can't let you go with me, Bobby."

Hurt and then indignation flashed across Bobby's face. "It's for your own good," Cass explained. "I can't let you do anything else that might jeopardize your job. As I recall, you're going to be putting yourself through school soon."

The boy nodded mutely.

"You can't afford to lose this job," Cass said soothingly. "I can't take the chance that you'll be penalized for doing the right thing in coming to me. I want you to promise you won't say anything about this to anyone else. I'll tell the police that my information came from a confidential source. With luck, Dr. Bellingham will suspect Mr. Howard slipped up somehow."

Bobby grinned. That particular possible consequence seemed to make Cass's alterations of his plan more palatable. "Okay," he agreed. "Do you know where Crosswhite Manor is?" Without waiting for her answer he plunged on. "It's not along the Cliff Walk, with the real famous places. It's out farther, next to Heritage Park. You can't see the house from the road—Mrs. Crosswhite has acres and acres—but you can't miss the spot. There's a high iron fence all around and a gatehouse out front with the name on it."

Cass nodded. "Thanks, Bobby. I can't tell you how much I appreciate everything you've done. If you hadn't figured all this out and then put your job on the line by telling me about it, I doubt I would ever have seen Crudley again. Now I think there is a good chance he'll be home very soon."

"He's a great cat, Miss Appleton," Bobby said. "If there's anything else I can do, you let me know." He stood up and threw a disgusted look back at the clinic. "I'm gonna start looking for another job, anyway. I don't like working here anymore. These animals have no class." He shoved his hands into the pockets of his low-slung jeans and exaggeratedly sauntered back to work.

Cass pulled out of the parking lot into rush-hour traffic. She should have taken a back way to Heritage Park, but on impulse she drove toward Bellevue Avenue. Her route would now take her past the renowned mansions Bobby had referred to. Perhaps looking at them first would make Crosswhite Manor seem less imposing.

When she'd first moved to Newport, Cass had behaved like a typical tourist. She'd strolled along the Cliff Walk, enjoying the panoramic ocean view on one side and the incredible architecture on the other. Along this one three-mile stretch of Atlantic coastline, she had seen some of the most opulent private homes, built around the turn of the century. The Breakers. Rosecliff. Marble House. The names evoked images of beauty and extravagance, money and imagination indulged and run wild. That had been Cass's first purely practical opinion.

But although the imitation European palaces, castles and châteaus were undeniably pretentious, Cass had come to think of them as oddly charming. Like the yearly yacht races and tennis tournaments, these flamboyant "summer cottages" belonged to a different era, or at least a different class than the one Cass inhabited. It seemed pointless to speculate about the motives and morality of the people who'd lived in such grandeur.

Except now Cass was forced to ask for help from one

of the residents of the great mansions. She fervently hoped that Bobby was right about this specific woman and that she was in fact "a nice person" and "pretty cool."

Nervously Cass practiced explaining the bizarre mix-up that had led to Crudley's kidnapping, and Mrs. Crosswhite's unintentional involvement in Cass's plight. Not until she pulled up the driveway in front of the heavy iron gates and saw the redbrick gatehouse manned by a private guard did Cass realize she had overlooked a fundamental problem. The guard eyed her neutrally, glanced conspicuously at a clipboard in his hand and then walked over to her car as she rolled down the window.

"Good day, ma'am," the guard said politely, just a hint of a foreign lilt adding music to his deep commanding voice. His eyes took in every detail of the interior of Cass's car as though she might be smuggling contraband. "Your name, please?"

"Cass Appleton," she told him. The guard studied his clipboard again. "Mrs. Crosswhite is not expecting me," Cass offered. "I didn't know I would have to come here today. It's an emergency. I only need to speak to her for a few minutes."

"Mrs. Crosswhite does not see anyone without an appointment," the guard said placidly.

"I can't make an appointment," Cass protested, growing frustrated. "Mrs. Crosswhite's telephone number is unlisted."

"That is because she does not like to be bothered by people she does not know."

For a moment the two of them stared at each other, neither willing to give an inch. Sweat trickled between Cass's shoulder blades, and she wondered how the guard managed to look so cool. Maybe it was all in the attitude. "Fine," Cass said eventually, raising her chin to look down her nose at the man, not an easy thing to do when she was sitting and he was towering over her. "Maybe I'll just wait here and catch her when she comes out."

"I would not advise that," the guard replied. "This driveway is private property. I am asking you to leave. If you do not, I will be forced to call the police. You could, of course, wait in the street if you choose, but the local authorities do not take kindly to people loitering in the area."

He wasn't bluffing. He had no need to make empty threats. He held all the cards and he knew it. Logic, duty and the law were on his side, and Cass was on the other. After a few seconds of glaring at the guard to prove he couldn't run her off, Cass threw the car into reverse and backed down the long, winding driveway to the street. Despite the guard's warning, she parked there for a few minutes, fuming.

She was annoyed at herself for not having anticipated the problem of getting in to see Mrs. Crosswhite. She should have realized visitors would be screened. On the other hand, what difference would it have made if she had thought about it ahead of time? She had a feeling the guard had heard every story in the book and didn't believe any of them. It would have come down to the same thing, one way or another: no appointment, no entrance, at least not through the front gate.

But surely there was another way in, Cass thought with sudden inspiration. The servants wouldn't use the front gate. Cass put the car in drive and headed slowly along the border of the Crosswhite acreage. She didn't remember passing another entrance, but she had been watching for the gatehouse. Almost a quarter of a mile from the main driveway, Cass spotted an unmarked service road. She turned into it and followed it for several hundred yards, stopping when she discovered a second massive iron gate, this one flanked by brick pylons, but no guardhouse. There was no sign of a guard, either, only a man digging in a nearby flower bed. The gardener, no doubt.

Cass parked the car and got out to examine the gate. She glanced at the gardener, who showed no interest in her arrival. Perhaps that was a good sign. Maybe people went in and out here all day without anyone noticing or caring. Cass pulled on the iron bars experimentally. The gate was definitely locked. Someone would have to open it for her from the other side.

She sneaked another peek at the gardener. Was he part of the permanent staff, or did Mrs. Crosswhite hire some landscaping service when she needed work done? Cass thought it over. A place this size would obviously have full-time year-round maintenance workers for the grounds. Her posing as one of the staff would be too risky; the gardener would probably know she was lying. Better to pretend to be a lost visitor coming to see Mrs. Crosswhite. That was sort of true, at least.

Cass took a few steps toward the gardener and called out, "Excuse me." The man continued working as though he hadn't heard her. With an easy rhythmic motion, he plunged his shovel again and again into the soft earth of the flower bed, deftly turning the soil as he lifted the blade out. He was drenched with sweat, yet his movements seemed almost effortless. A natural animal grace marked every aspect of his activity. His T-shirt had been cast onto the nearby grass. For a moment Cass stood mesmerized by the play of muscles across the man's broad shoulders and back, the gleam of his bronzed skin.

With an effort she shook off her trance and walked closer to him, following the heavy ornamental iron fence a short distance until she was only a few feet from the man. "Excuse me," she repeated, louder than before.

This time, the gardener must have heard her. He drove his shovel into the ground and turned toward Cass. Involuntarily she caught her breath. He was incredibly good-looking. Her next thought was that he'd probably been a beautiful child. The years had sculpted a leaner, more angular look to his cheekbones and jawline, and added enough experience to make the face even more interesting than it was handsome. His sea green eyes regarded her with polite inquiry, the proper attitude, she supposed, for the hired help. Cass wished she felt equally unaffected by him. She was here on business, after all.

She cleared her throat. "Would you help me, please?" she asked. She tried to sound imperious, like a lady of the manor used to ordering the servants about. Instead, her uncertain delivery gave the request a peculiar poignance rather than any insistence.

The gardener leaned on his shovel, one foot propped on the blade. "What can I do for you?" he asked.

"I'm here to see Mrs. Crosswhite. Would you please let me in?" Cass pointed to the huge wrought iron gate.

"The main gate is back that way." The gardener jerked his head in the direction she'd just come from. "Security there screens all visitors."

"I know. I was already there. He... There wasn't anyone at the gate so I came around here." Cass had thought it wasn't possible to feel any more overheated and uncomfortable until hot blood flooded her cheeks with the lie. She tugged at the neckline of her wilting silk blouse, trying to unstick the material from her perspiring skin.

"The front gate is always manned," the gardener said, watching Cass squirm as he calmly confronted her with her own falsehood.

Cass pushed a wet tendril of dark hair out of her eyes. She had no patience for this kind of game. "All right," she admitted. "Someone was there. He wouldn't let me in. He insisted I had to make an appointment first, but I can't make an appointment because Mrs. Crosswhite's phone number is unlisted and I haven't time to write a letter. It's vitally important that I speak with Mrs. Crosswhite. If I could just explain the problem to her..."

"Explain it to me."

The gardener walked casually toward Cass, pulling off his heavy gloves. He stopped just on the other side of the fence, disconcertingly close. Cass could smell the mingled scents of earth and grass clinging to his sweat-sheened body. The sun glinted off his streaked sandy brown hair.

"Explain it to you?" Cass repeated.

"Explain it to me. Convince me you need to see Mrs. Crosswhite and maybe I'll let you in."

Cass didn't like the direct way he looked into her eyes, or the keen intelligence evident in his coolly assessing gaze. He seemed to be taking her measure in a completely detached, analytical way that was more intimidating and more intimate than the leering and ogling some men indulged in. She felt exposed and vulnerable, as though all her secrets were being laid bare before his critical eye. She took a step backward and folded her arms protectively across her breasts, forcing herself to meet his stare. "I can't," she said. "It's personal."

Gabe Preston had assessed the woman on the far side of the fence with a single, trained glance. Now he made a show of giving her a slow once-over, head to toe, just to see how she'd react. Nice legs, he thought fleetingly, as she reflexively retreated a step or two despite the obvious protection of the wrought iron gate standing between them.

Everything about her was all wrong. Her dressed-for-success suit was damp and wrinkled with heat and perspiration, but the style was a mistake in any case. The straight, clean lines of the short jacket and slim skirt had trouble accommodating the lush curves of her body which spoiled the intended silhouette.

The haircut was equally amiss. Some hair stylist's fantasy of sleek sophistication, it clearly was supposed to have a sculpted appearance. Instead, her thick, dark hair was windblown and tousled. It curled and waved around her face damply, destroying the elegant simplicity she probably hoped for.

In short, she was a mess, albeit an attractive one, right down to the guarded but obviously distressed expression in her hazel eyes. Gabe was intrigued in spite of himself. "I can't help you if you don't tell me what it's about," he advised her.

Was Cass only imagining a change in his voice or did he really sound concerned now? Here was her opportunity, yet she balked at telling her story to a stranger. He would think her ridiculous and no doubt refuse to help.

"I can only say it's urgent," she hedged. "A matter of life and death, really. Please, won't you let me in?" She read surprise and doubt but also hesitation in his unguarded eyes. Desperately she searched for a way to tip the balance in her favor. "I...I'll pay you," she added, fumbling at the catch of her purse.

For a moment the gardener looked stunned. Then he threw back his head and roared with laughter.

Cass didn't understand what he found so funny. Did Mrs. Crosswhite pay this man so well he didn't need any extra money, or was it the notion that Cass could have enough in her purse to interest him that he found so hilarious? Regardless, she seemed to have forfeited what little headway she'd made. Any spark of compassion she might have glimpsed in the gardener's eyes had been extinguished by amusement. She snapped her purse shut.

"Excuse me," the man said, recovering himself and taking note of Cass's stony expression. "I suppose that must seem like a logical offer to you. And it probably sounds hypocritical to say, standing in front of a place like this—" his arm made a sweeping gesture encompassing the estate grounds "—that money can't buy everything. But it can't, you know. That's the first thing you learn when you're around people who have lots of it."

He leaned against the wrought iron bars of the fence, so close Cass could hear him breathe. He lowered his voice to acknowledge their new proximity. "Money is also no guarantee of sincerity, I'm afraid. No," he said, shaking his head, "you'll have to find some other way to convince me to let you in." Then he made a deliberate show of giving her a slow once-over, head to toe, and grinned wickedly as he met her gaze.

Chapter Two

Cass glowered at the smiling gardener, trying without success to ignore the physical sensations that flooded through her body when she looked into his laughing green eyes. She was certain she knew exactly what this man expected her to offer by way of a bribe.

She wasn't willing to go that far to see Mrs. Crosswhite. There had to be some other way to get inside the fence. But before she left this gate, admitting temporary defeat, she could still salvage a minor triumph. It would be a real pleasure to slap the smirk off the gardener's face. "Just what do you have in mind?" she asked with studied innocence.

'Well..." the man stepped back and made another exaggerated survey of her through half-closed eyes veiled by dark lashes. He smiled slowly. "You could climb the fence."

Cass stared at him, uncomprehending, so prepared for him to say something else that she could muster no response to what he actually said.

"You see," he continued, "if I were to go back to my digging and you were to climb the fence while I wasn't looking, then you could say that you'd become lost on the way to the house, and I'd have to show you there. It wouldn't be as though I'd actually let you in. Once you're on the grounds, you're presumed to be a guest and I'd have to show you every courtesy." The gardener's grin was even wider now, and more knowing. He'd guessed the kind of proposition Cass expected and was enjoying her speechless confusion.

His smug good humor irritated her, not least because she knew how unfairly she'd judged him. She'd taken for granted he felt the same physical attraction that kept intruding, unbidden, into her own thoughts. Then she'd compounded that error by assuming he was the sort of man to take advantage of a woman in a difficult situation.

Cass narrowed her eyes in deliberation as she studied first the tall iron fence, then the gardener. If he was on a power trip, it was different from anything she'd seen before. He looked more like a kid who'd just dared his best friend to try something that would get them both in trouble. She glanced at the fence again. From the corner of her eye she saw the gardener's eyebrows lift, as if he didn't really believe she would even consider his bizarre proposal.

Cass took off her shoes and thrust them through the iron bars at the gardener. "Hold these," she instructed, handing him her purse next, then shedding the boxy jacket of her suit. She hitched her skirt up to midthigh. Giving one last peek at the gardener's astonished face, she proceeded to scale the fence with easy athletic grace. At the top she hiked her skirt higher and held on to it with one hand while she jumped down onto the grass of the Crosswhite estate, landing lightly with a deep flex of her knees.

She stood up, dusting imaginary grass stains from her hands, then walked over to the gardener. "Thank you," she said as she retrieved her clothes and put on her low-heeled pumps.

The gardener laughed again. This time Cass felt oddly pleased to have provoked the rich tenor explosion of delight.

"I can see you didn't misspend your youth in smoky pool halls," he said. "You must have been the local tomboy."

"I still am," Cass said proudly, defying him to contradict her. Her heart had begun pounding in delayed reaction to her reckless act.

"You'll get no argument from me," he said. He threw his hands up in a gesture of surrender.

"Good. Then just tell me where to find Mrs. Crosswhite and you can go back to what you were doing."

He reached for the white T-shirt lying on the grass and quickly pulled it on. "I'm afraid it's not that simple," he began.

Cass bridled instantly. "What? I thought we had a deal? You said—"

"Easy, girl, easy! I'm not reneging. I'm just trying to explain to you that I have to go with you. You'll never find Emilie without a guide. Any of her employees would toss you out before you had a chance to look for her unless you're with someone they know. They're a very protective bunch. So stick with me, and I'll do all the talking if anyone stops us. Got it?"

"Got it," Cass said, tucking her damp blouse back into the equally damp waistband of her skirt. She decided to carry her jacket, at least until they reached the house.

"Good." The gardener reached for her hand and tugged lightly to start her moving. He kept hold of her hand as they walked, even though it was clear to Cass they were simply heading in a straight line across the grassy expanse of lawn toward the imposing manor house. The huge hand enveloping hers comforted Cass, like a promise of safe passage through the terrors of life. She felt a surge of optimism. She had made it inside the gates. She was going to see Mrs. Crosswhite. Everything could work out, after all.

They came up on the rear of the house, threading their way through an elaborate English-style garden with a maze of box hedges. They crossed a broad brick patio to a set of French doors, which the gardener pulled open, gesturing for Cass to go inside. She hesitated, watching him kneel down to unlace and kick off his boots before entering the house himself.

Once inside he crossed rapidly to a wall phone and picked it up, not bothering to dial. A few moments later he said, "Mark? I'm in the morning room. Would you ask Emilie to meet me here? I've brought her an unexpected guest."

The morning room. That was a good name for it. It would be even more impressive in the early hours of the day than it was now in late afternoon. Huge windows and glass doors allowed the sunlight to bathe every corner. Beautiful healthy-looking plants flaunted their rainbow hues everywhere—tall ones standing in pots on the floor, smaller ones resting on tables or hanging in baskets from overhead hooks. White wicker furniture accented with overstuffed cushions in a green and yellow floral pattern completed the motif. Cass could have believed she was standing in a furnished greenhouse, except the air was deliciously cool.

The gardener hung up the phone and flopped into one

of the flowered chairs. "Make yourself comfortable," he said.

Comfort was an impossibility at that moment, despite the cultivated charm of the room. Cass was too worried about her impending interview with Mrs. Crosswhite. She tried to mentally compose herself, but found herself distracted by questions about the man who had brought her this far in her quest to rescue Crudley. He'd twice referred to Mrs Crosswhite as "Emilie." The first time, Cass had dismissed it, assuming he was being flippant about his employer in the way many employees are when the boss is out of earshot. Now she was forced to consider whether she had completely mistaken this man's function at Crosswhite Manor and his relationship with its owner.

He seemed perfectly at ease inside the residence. He'd let himself in without a second's thought, removing his boots first with what might be interpreted as proprietary care. He knew where the house phone was and used it to issue a rather peremptory summons for Mrs. Crosswhite. Now he lounged casually in a chair, awaiting the great lady's arrival while encouraging Cass to make herself comfortable, too, as though he had every right to bring anyone into this house on any terms he chose. Who was he?

Cass licked her lips nervously. At this point he was her only ally. She'd tried lying to him, ordering him around and finally bribing him to worm her way inside the gate. He'd laughed all that off and helped her, anyway. Would he have let her in the gate if she hadn't taken up his ridiculous challenge to scale the fence? She had no clue. It made her uneasy, though, having to worry about his motives and his pull with the woman whose help she'd come to request.

Cass pulled on the jacket to her suit and smoothed it

as best she could, then ran her fingers through her wildly disarrayed hair trying to restore it to some semblance of neatness. She perched carefully on the edge of a chair and flicked a quick look at her guide. He was watching her with continuing frank amusement. She suppressed her irritation and forced herself to meet his laughing eyes. "Thank you for helping me," she said.

He shrugged. "We had a deal. Maybe you'd better tell me your name, though. It will make the introductions easier when Emilie arrives."

"Cass Appleton."

"Gabe Preston. Nice to meet you."

She nodded, then they lapsed into silence for several minutes.

The door opened abruptly. A tiny white-haired woman floated in wearing a long silvery gown that made her look like an earthbound cherub. She turned immediately to the gardener, who'd risen automatically at the sound of her arrival. "Gabriel, darling," she said, lifting her smooth powdered cheek for a kiss.

"Hi, Emilie." He gave her a hug along with the kiss.

The woman turned quickly to Cass, who also stood automatically. "And you've brought a guest. How wonderful." She drifted forward as though she were walking on a cloud, her hand outstretched to grasp Cass's. "It's so lovely to meet one of Gabriel's friends."

"She's here to see you, Emilie," Gabe explained. "I just happened to meet her on the grounds, so I showed her the way to the house. Emilie, this is Cass Appleton. Cass, Emilie Crosswhite."

"You're here to see me?" Emilie Crosswhite repeated, turning to Gabe while clinging to Cass's hand. "I thought I didn't have any appointments this afternoon."

"I don't have an appointment, Mrs. Crosswhite," Cass

confessed, releasing the tiny cool hand that had gripped hers with unexpected firmness. "I didn't have time to make one. I'm here because of an emergency."

"An emergency!" Mrs. Crosswhite's clear blue eyes dimmed with concern. Her classically arched eyebrows drew together as she frowned. "Sit down, my dear. Gabriel, ring for tea, won't you please?" She led Cass to a sofa and sat, patting the cushion next to her. "Tell me all about it."

Cass sat and her eyes flicked toward Gabe, who was speaking on the house phone. "It's rather personal," she said softly.

Mrs. Crosswhite followed the direction of her glance. "You mustn't worry about Gabriel, my dear. He's my godson and my most trusted friend. I have no secrets from him." She laughed gaily, like a girl. "Except my age of course. No one knows that but me, and I'm afraid I've quite forgotten it."

Gabriel had hung up the phone and stood propped against a high-backed chair, his forearms resting lightly on the wicker. His sea green eyes were alert and watchful, belying the casual pose.

Cass took a deep breath. "I'm not sure I know where to begin."

Emilie Crosswhite patted her hand. "Just take your time, dear, and do the best you can. Gabriel will explain it to me if I don't understand at first."

That wasn't a reassuring thought. Cass turned so she wouldn't have to see Gabe's face when she told Mrs. Crosswhite the reason for her visit. "Someone has kidnapped my cat," she said.

"Oh, my dear!" Mrs. Crosswhite exclaimed, genuine distress clear on her face. "How awful for you."

Cass ignored the choking snorting sounds coming from

Gabe Preston's direction and concentrated on capitalizing on Mrs. Crosswhite's sympathy. "They didn't mean to take my cat. They meant to take your cat, Princess Athabasca."

"My cat?" Emilie Crosswhite looked confused. She shot a quick look at Gabe, searching for a clue to Cass's mysterious statement. Apparently he was no help. She focused on Cass again. "I don't understand, dear."

"There was a burglary at Dr. Bellingham's clinic last night," Cass explained. "Whoever broke in took my cat and left a note. The note said the kidnappers would be calling you tonight to give you instructions on when and where to leave the ransom money. They think they stole Princess Athabasca, but they made a mistake and took the wrong cat. *My* cat."

"That is the most ridiculous—" Gabe began.

Emilie Crosswhite brought him up short with a stern look, then addressed Cass. "What does your cat look like, dear?"

"He's a big gray tom with gold eyes. Bobby, one of the kennel boys who works for Dr. Bellingham, says there's a strong superficial resemblance between Crudley and the Princess."

"Crudley?" Gabe echoed in disbelief. Cass nodded without looking at him. For the first time she wished she'd given her cat a more impressive name.

Emilie, however, seemed quite taken with the name. "That would be," she ventured, "*C-r-u-d-l-e-i-g-h?* He is French, isn't he?"

The unmistakable twinkle in Emilie Crosswhite's eyes filled Cass with renewed hope. She smiled and shook her head in answer. "No, he's American. It's just plain *l-e-y.*"

"How refreshing! And what a relief, really. The French

can be so fiercely independent one hesitates to offer help. A French cat, no matter how desperate his straits, might very well try to bite the hand that rescued him. I speak with some authority. We had a French poodle once—"

"Emilie," Gabe interrupted, his voice dropping to a lower warning register.

"Now, Gabriel," Emilie Crosswhite answered him, a hint of willfulness in her tone, "you know we have to help the girl."

"This is not your problem," he insisted.

"Of course it is," she countered. "Someone tried to kidnap Princess Athabasca. They failed, but only because this girl's brave cat thwarted their plans by valiantly substituting himself for their intended victim. It could easily be the Princess and not poor Crudley languishing in a cold dark cage somewhere without food or water or a kind voice to cheer him."

Gabe rolled his eyes theatrically and crossed his arms over his broad chest. "Emilie, your whimsical interpretation of events is an *almost* constant delight to me. But in this case, I think you're overreacting. This woman is a stranger. She showed up here today unannounced, charmed her way past the staff—" he had the grace to stumble a little over that "—and now she's trying to sell you this preposterous story, apparently in the hope you'll feel guilty and agree to pay off some alleged kidnappers for the return of a cat she may or may not even own."

Cass was prepared to take offense when Emilie Crosswhite took it for her. "Now who's being ridiculous?" the older woman demanded. "No one would name an imaginary cat 'Crudley.' He's obviously a real cat, and he's obviously an innocent bystander, caught up in a plot to extort money from me. I cannot simply abandon this poor animal or pretend I bear no responsibility for what happens to him. He would be safe at this moment if I hadn't taken the Princess to that wretched clinic for her yearly tonic."

Cass had a fleeting vision of a kitty health spa where overweight and overpampered cats dined on caviar and drank Perrier water while attendants brushed their fur and clipped their unused claws. Then Gabe rejoined the argument. "What if she does own a cat named Crudley? What if he was at Dr. Bellingham's clinic last night and he's missing now? How do you know this woman isn't the extortionist herself? How do you know she didn't come here today to give you this sob story in person just to convince you to pay the ransom?"

"Very simply," Cass interrupted, her temper rising at Gabe's about-face and his attempt to blacken her character. "You know that isn't true because I didn't come here to ask Mrs. Crosswhite for any money."

Emilie Crosswhite beamed at Cass, then threw a smug little smile in Gabe's direction. "You see?" she scolded him. "I keep telling you not to assume the worst about people."

Gabriel Preston colored deeply, an unreadable mix of emotions flashing across his face. He wasn't ready to surrender, however. "Why did you come here, then?" he demanded of Cass.

"To ask Mrs. Crosswhite if she'd help by stalling the kidnappers when they call." She turned to Emilie. "If you could play along with them, tell them you need time to collect the ransom and most of all *not* tell them they have the wrong cat, then that will give me a chance to notify the police. They can set up a phone trace or something and catch the people who did this."

"The police are not going to go to all that trouble because of a missing cat," Gabe interjected.

"He's not missing. He was stolen," Cass corrected hotly.

"Even if he was," Gabe said wearily, "that isn't a crime."

"Of course it's a crime!"

Gabe shook his head. "Cats are not considered property in this county."

The two women stared at him, uncomprehending. "What does that mean?" Cass finally demanded.

"It means cats can't be 'stolen' because legally they don't belong to anyone. They're like squirrels or raccoons."

Emilie waved off Gabe's statement. "They're not a bit like either of those creatures."

"Legally speaking, Emilie, cats are considered no different from wild animals. Unless they're living on a game preserve, protected by state or federal government, their welfare falls outside the scope of the law."

"But that's absurd—"

"I never heard of anything—"

Both women had spoken at once. Both broke off at the same time, silently considering the implication of Gabe's words. Cass found her voice first. "What about the break-in at the clinic? Isn't that a crime?"

"Of course," Gabe acknowledged. "And if the doctor notifies the police, they'll take a report and conduct a routine investigation. They aren't going to hunt for a missing cat, though."

Cass's jaw muscles tightened. "What about the ransom note? What happens when the kidnappers call and demand money from Mrs. Crosswhite? Isn't that a crime?"

"Yes, that's a crime, too. If anyone tries to extort money from Emilie, naturally she'll report it to the police. But once she tells the extortionists they don't have her cat and she won't pay them a dime, she won't have any further contact with them."

"And what happens to my cat if she tells them that?"

Gabe shrugged. "Whoever took him, if someone really did take him, will probably just let him go." He grinned wryly. "It isn't as though the kidnappers have to worry about your cat identifying them to the authorities. There's no reason for them to hurt Crudley."

"So they'll dump him somewhere and I'll never see him again and then everything will be fine. Is that right?" Cass challenged.

Gabe had no answer. Silence fell on the group until Emilie Crosswhite gradually emerged from the fog of thoughtfulness that had enveloped her. "I cannot believe," she said, "that the Princess could have been kidnapped and the police would do nothing to save her." She made a nervous fluttery gesture with one hand.

"That would be a completely different situation, Emilie," Gabe hastened to assure her. "If the Princess had been taken, there would certainly be an investigation."

Emilie looked from Gabe's calm face to Cass's bewildered one as though afraid she was the only one who didn't understand. "I thought you said the police wouldn't consider a cat stolen."

"The Princess is a show cat, Emilie. She has monetary, not just sentimental value. The law recognizes that."

"Oh." Emilie relaxed slightly even as Cass stiffened with anger. "Oh!" Emilie repeated with new distress as the meaning of Gabe's analysis sunk in. She glanced at Cass's tight-lipped profile. "Oh, dear. That really isn't fair at all."

Gabe quirked up one corner of his mouth and raised his eyebrows as if to say, *What else is new?*

Cass shot an angry look at him. "I'm sure you believed

it when you said money can't buy everything, Mr. Preston. You forgot to add, though, that a lack of money buys even less."

Cass rose to go, infuriated that none of the sacrifices she made ever seemed to be enough. Money remained the great unequalizer. The world was run by the rich, for the benefit of the rich. Only they could expect "fair" treatment. Only they had the kind of security she'd worked so desperately to create for herself.

Emilie Crosswhite laid a surprisingly firm hand on Cass's knee, pressing her to stay seated. She thrust her small but determined chin forward. "Well, Gabriel," she announced, "if the police won't help this girl, we certainly must."

Gabe fixed Emilie with a warning look. "Now, Emilie..."

"Now, Gabriel..."

"What is it you propose to do?"

"I don't know yet. You'll have to help me figure that out. But it must be something that brings Crudley home safe to Miss Appleton." Emilie patted Cass's knee to emphasize her comforting words.

"You can't mean you want to cooperate with these alleged kidnappers?" Gabe said incredulously.

"If that's what it takes."

Gabe threw up his hands in disgust. "Oh, for Pete's sake, Emilie! Do you seriously believe Mark Gallagher will allow you to write a blank check to pay off some bungling extortionists who can't even snatch the right cat?"

"He's a wonderful advisor, but it's my money," Emilie insisted serenely. "I don't see how he can stop me."

"Emilie, you know very well—"

"Gabriel, I adore you but—"

"Excuse me," Cass said, "but I already told you I didn't want—"

The phone jangled loudly, arresting the verbal free-for-all. The three combatants stared at the white instrument perched on the wicker table as it rang again. Emilie Crosswhite and Gabe Preston moved toward it together until Emilie halted Gabe with an imperious look. She picked up the receiver and spoke calmly into it. "Yes, Mark?"

Emilie turned to smile at Cass, pointedly ignoring Gabe who stood, hulking over her, apparently trying to look menacing. "Put him through, dear," she said. For the next few moments she concentrated on her conversation. "Yes...yes, I do... I see... Well, of course I do... No, no I wouldn't do that... Is he, er, she all right?... Good, because if anything were to happen to him, uh, her, naturally I wouldn't pay... Yes, I understand... Yes... Well, that's quite a lot of money—not the sort of sum I have just lying about the house. I'll need a few days to make arrangements to have it ready.... No, that would be quite impossible. I'll need until Friday at least— Friday, that's right... Very well." Emilie hung up the phone and turned to her expectant audience.

Emilie still ignored Gabe and looked at Cass, breaking into a triumphant grin as she did. "They're giving us until Friday. I told them I couldn't possibly have the money before then. That gives us three whole days to come up with a plan."

Gabe took a quick step to Emilie's side. "What kind of plan?"

"The police may not be interested in our problem now," she said haughtily, "but once we capture the catnappers and hand them over, I assure you the authorities will take us seriously."

Cass could hardly fail to notice she seemed to have

acquired a new ally. Neither could Gabe. "This has gone far enough, Emilie. Despite my advice, you've done all Miss Appleton claims she wanted you to. You've stalled the kidnappers. Now stay out of it."

Emilie shook her head determinedly. "She was counting on the police to help her after I'd done my small part. But as you've so logically explained, they won't. I'll have to, instead."

Gabe stared into Emilie's unwavering blue eyes. Sighing heavily, he ran his fingers through his sun-streaked hair. "Just how do you two amateur detectives propose to catch these crooks? Where are you going to begin your investigation?"

Emilie flicked a glance at Cass, who could only look back blankly. Her meeting with the society matron hadn't gone quite as she'd hoped. She'd never planned on doing any investigating on her own. She'd expected to turn the whole mess over to the police. Suddenly left to her own devices, she hadn't a clue what to do next. She shrugged and bit her lip. "We'll think of something," she said lamely.

Emilie Crosswhite was not so easily daunted. She looked Gabe square in the eye and smiled engagingly, as though they hadn't been arguing ten seconds before. "You could help us," she said sweetly.

"No." The softness of the immediate response did nothing to lessen its forcefulness. Gabe picked up Emilie's tiny fragile hand and held it tenderly in his own. "You know I can't. And you know why."

For a long moment the two of them looked at each other as though conducting a private conversation in complete silence. Emilie patted Gabe's hand and smiled pensively. "I know, dear." She turned back to Cass. "I suppose we'll just have to pay the ransom."

"What?" Gabe and Cass chorused with varying degrees of surprise.

"I don't see any other choice," Emilie said to Cass. "And it's only ten thousand dollars," she said to Gabe, adding with a meaningful lift of one eyebrow. "Hardly worth arguing about."

"Ten thousand dollars?" Cass echoed. Unlike Emilie Crosswhite, she was horrified at the thought of spending so much money in a lump sum for anything. At the same time she was relieved that complying with the kidnappers' demands would not be impossible, after all.

"Ten thousand dollars?" Gabe repeated in turn. "Are you sure that's what they said?"

"Ten thousand dollars," Emilie confirmed. "Since you won't help us capture the kidnappers, we'll just have to pay them off. I would have given them ten times that amount to secure Princess Athabasca's return."

"I know," Gabe said. He frowned in confusion. "It's almost as though whoever planned to take her doesn't understand how much she's really worth. I don't like it."

Cass stared at him in amazement. "I don't believe you! A minute ago you were insisting Mrs. Crosswhite not pay anything, and now you're insulted because they've asked for too *little* money!"

Gabe conceded the seeming oddness of his remark with a wry smile. "Not exactly. I am worried, though, that whoever stole your cat doesn't have a better grasp of what its market value should be."

"Worry all you like," Cass replied in exasperation. "Personally I'm thrilled. If they'd demanded any more, I would never have been able to pay. As it is, by emptying my bank account and floating a small cash loan on my credit card, I can come up with the ransom."

"Now, dear, you shouldn't have to spend your life's

savings, even for such a worthy cause as rescuing your beloved pet. When I agreed to the kidnappers' terms without consulting you, I made myself responsible for paying. I had no intention of forcing you to accept the financial burden."

"That's very generous of you, Mrs. Crosswhite. But I already explained I didn't come here to ask for money. You've been very kind. Without your help I don't know what I would have done. This isn't how I expected to save my cat, but it doesn't matter as long as he comes home safely."

"Just a minute," Gabe said, completely frustrated by the rapid turn of events. "You seem to have forgotten one or two minor details. Who is going to deliver the ransom money to the kidnappers? Where? When? These kinds of transactions don't usually occur in broad daylight in public places. There is bound to be some danger to the person carrying the money."

"He's my cat. It's my money. I'll make the delivery," Cass said shortly.

"And what if they want Emilie herself to be the courier?"

"Then I will be," Emilie chimed in.

Cass threw an uneasy glance at the tiny woman. "We'll cross that bridge when we come to it. If we come to it," she said with more confidence than she felt. "Look, all these people want is the money. They don't want trouble. Why are you looking for problems where there are none?"

Gabe sighed heavily. "The problems are there whether or not you choose to see them. I already told you, the relatively small ransom the thieves have demanded means something. The only possibilities I can think of aren't good. Most likely, it means we're dealing with amateurs who don't understand the value of what they've stolen. As amateurs, they'll be twice as dangerous as professional crooks. They'll be nervous and unpredictable, easily frightened into doing something stupid that could hurt someone. They'll make mistakes and, unfortunately, you could be the ones to suffer for it."

The women silently thought over Gabe's analysis. Cass shifted uneasily on the wicker sofa. "There could be other explanations for why they asked for that particular amount of money," she said.

"Perhaps ten thousand dollars is all they need," Emilie suggested.

Gabe smiled tolerantly. "Greed, not need, usually motivates a kidnapper, Emilie. Maybe this first demand is only a way to test the waters. Maybe when the kidnappers call back Friday they'll ask for twice as much. Or ten times as much. Maybe this is a kind of training exercise for them. Maybe they plan to go into business kidnapping the pets of wealthy people and ransoming them back. It's a lot safer than kidnapping people, and could be almost as lucrative if you pick the right victim."

He spread his hands and lifted his palms to indicate the world of possibilities. "I don't know. But that's my point. None of us understand the kidnappers' motives, beyond the obvious desire to acquire some of somebody else's money. My concern—" he leveled a serious expression at Emilie Crosswhite "—is you, Emilie. I can't let you endanger yourself. That would be completely irresponsible of me."

Emilie gazed at him fondly for a few moments. "I know, dear," she said. "But my mind is quite made up. I intend to help Miss Appleton recover Crudley. You'll just have to find a way to keep all three of us out of danger." Gabe shook his head and rolled his eyes heavenward. Emilie leaned toward Cass and confided in a loud whisper, "That means he knows he's lost the argument."

"I heard that," Gabe announced. "And contrary to your interpretation, all it really means is that I'm willing to call a temporary truce. I'm not making any commitments. You're not making any commitments, Emilie. But Miss Appleton says she has the money. The kidnappers are supposed to call back Friday with further instructions. We'll wait and see what they have to say."

"That's all we ask, dear," Emilie assured him soberly while giving Cass a surreptitious wink.

As if on cue, a servant entered carrying a tray with three glasses of iced tea. The timing made Cass suspect the woman had been listening at the door, waiting for a break in the conversation. A second look at the woman's elegant dress and regal bearing caused Cass to reconsider. She was hardly the type to eavesdrop. Her manner was deferential, but not the least bit servile. Tall and slender, she had the same smooth caramel complexion and piercing amber eyes of the gate guard. The two employees had to be related.

Tempting as the iced tea looked, Cass decided to take advantage of the natural break in events to leave. "Well," she said, standing and ineffectually trying to smooth her wrinkled skirt, "I've taken enough of your time. I should be going. Despite Mr. Preston's conviction that the police won't be interested, I'd still like to stop by the station and make a report."

"Suit yourself," Gabe said with apparent indifference.

"I think that's a fine idea," Mrs. Crosswhite said. "And if you think it will help poor Crudley at all, be sure and tell the police that you've spoken to Gabriel and me and we're willing to cooperate in every way."

Gabe tensed at this suggestion and came dangerously

Chapter Three

Outside, the heat seemed more intense than before. Where were Newport's famed cooling ocean breezes?

Cass trailed her swift-moving escort back across the broad green lawns to the service road. By the time they reached the rear gate, Cass felt wilted all over again. "I hope you remembered to bring the key," she said irritably. "I don't feel like leaving the same way I came in."

Gabe ignored her tone and stepped to one of the brick stanchions flanking the thick iron gate. Deftly he exposed a hidden control panel and punched in a coded number sequence. The heavy metal grillwork slid smoothly back.

Cass regarded her guide with a fresh flare of anger. "You knew all along how to open the gate. Why did you make me climb that fence?"

Gabe met her hostility impassively. "I needed to confirm my suspicions."

"Well, I'm sorry to disappoint you," Cass said with a superior tone.

close to scowling at his employer. "I'll show Miss Appleton out," he said curtly, striding to the door and waiting with obvious impatience as Cass thanked Emilie Crosswhite one final time.

"You didn't disappoint me at all. I suspected you had great legs, and you do."

The unexpected turn of the conversation flustered Cass completely, as she was sure Gabe had intended. He was probably still testing her, hoping to provoke some revealing reaction. She wheeled and stalked through the gate.

Gabe caught her before she'd taken two steps, grasping her wrist gently but firmly to pull her up short. "I had to know how serious you were about needing to see Emilie," he said unapologetically. "It's your own fault," he added. "You refused to tell me what was going on."

"Oh, right. I'm sure if I *had* told you that my cat was mistakenly kidnapped, you would have flung the gates wide and happily ushered me in."

"You'll never know now, will you?"

"I can make a pretty good guess, based on the way you acted up at the house. I would never have been permitted within a mile of Mrs. Crosswhite."

"Maybe not. Just remember, I don't have to justify my conduct to you. I'm not only Emilie's godson and friend, I'm also chief of security for Crosswhite Enterprises. I'm certainly not going to defend myself for wanting to protect Emilie from the con artists and opportunists who've been trying to get at her ever since her husband died."

"Con artists? Opportunists?" Cass bridled. "You have no right to lump me in with people like that. I work for a living. I pay my own way. I came here to ask for the smallest of favors—a little of Emilie Crosswhite's time and an inconsequential delay in telling the kidnappers they goofed. I'm the only one who's been taken advantage of."

"Maybe."

"What is that supposed to mean?"

"Just that I'm reserving judgment until this scenario has played itself out. Completely."

"I don't expect you to be around for the finish. Once I have the ransom instructions, I'll gladly disappear from your life. What happens after that is between me and the kidnappers. It won't concern you or Mrs. Crosswhite."

"I hope you're right. I hope you don't give me any reason to regret the impulse to let you in here today."

"What are you talking about?" Cass demanded in exasperation.

Gabe stared at her for a long moment, making his face an unreadable mask. "Let's pretend," he said evenly, "that you weren't strictly on the up-and-up. Let's say that you wanted to win Emilie's confidence, and her sympathy. You might come to her with a story exactly like the one you told today. You're an innocent bystander, caught up in a bungled extortion attempt. Fortunately you have just enough money to meet the kidnappers' demands.

"Then on the day the exchange is to take place, and at the very last minute, the crooks demand more money. You're totally tapped out. You've mortgaged your soul to scrape together the ten thousand they originally wanted. Tears and hand-wringing. What are you to do? Oh, happy day! Mrs. Emilie Crosswhite, noted philanthropist with enough money to pay the ransom a thousand times over, steps in quickly to offer assistance. Whether you let her give you the money or force her to accept a promise of repayment, the result is the same. You and the money and the phantom kidnapped cat vanish forever."

Cass jerked her wrist out of Gabe's fingers. Angry color mottled her cheeks. "That's a very convincing story, Mr. Preston," she said tightly. "Except that my cat is not a phantom and I am not a thief. If you're really worried about people taking advantage of Mrs. Crosswhite, I suggest you look in the mirror. You're a little too familiar with the worst in human nature. You might ask yourself why."

"My character is not in question," he said softly.

"And mine is?" Cass challenged.

Gabe raised one shoulder and tilted his head to regard her speculatively. He didn't answer.

Cass reached for her car door, brushing aside Gabe's attempt to open it for her. With an unnecessary roar, she started the vehicle and backed down the road. Her last view of the Crosswhite estate showed the enigmatic figure of Gabe Preston framed between the pillars in the high iron fence.

Over an hour later Cass walked in the front door of her carriage-house apartment and twisted around to lock it behind her with a well-practiced fluid motion. Today the act seemed more symbolic than practical. She wanted to shut out everything that had happened.

Dumping the grocery bag on the counter, she kicked off her shoes, shrugged out of her linen jacket and was all but undressed by the time she entered the bedroom only seconds later. She tossed her clothing into a hamper of clothes intended for dry cleaning and rapidly donned a T-shirt and denim cutoffs. Tying back her hair, she scrubbed off the sticky remnants of makeup that had somehow survived the day.

For a moment she almost felt safe. She was home. The apartment was small, but efficiently designed, and everywhere reflected touches of her personality. She could have afforded a larger place in a less pricey section of town, but that would have meant sacrificing the prestige of her current address, a rare rental in a neighborhood noted for its older, distinguished and definitely upscale homes. Cass had been lucky to find her place. It allowed her to maintain the illusion of discreet affluence her employers valued. It also allowed her to save a relatively large portion of her all too discreet salary, so that in a little over two years with the firm, she'd managed to save nearly ten thousand dollars.

Cass tried not to think about how soon the money would be gone, tried not to feel that she'd wasted an entire two years as an accountant at Laughlin and Denmore accumulating her nest egg. She was lucky to have the money when she needed it. After all, that was its purpose—to buy security. She was fortunate the kidnappers hadn't asked for more. She refused even to consider Gabe Preston's theory that this demand for cash might be only the first installment in an ongoing, more expensive extortion scheme.

She would not dwell on depressing thoughts like that. Walking into the kitchen, she busied herself with preparations for dinner. After she'd eaten a few bites of food, she felt herself begin to relax. For a brief time she concentrated on the smell and taste and texture of the rich cheesy macaroni. She hadn't realized how tired or how hungry she was. She'd been on the run for almost four days straight, her weekend a total loss as she'd had to meet with a client in Louisville, Kentucky, and give him the latest figures for his taxes.

As if that hadn't been enough, she'd arrived at the veterinarian's to find Crudley had apparently escaped. Barely recovered from that shock, she'd learned he hadn't escaped but been kidnapped, the victim of mistaken identity. She had driven all the way to Crosswhite Manor, climbed a fence and exposed her troubles to a complete stranger. And the result of the whole ridiculous meeting with Emilie Crosswhite and her chief of security was that she might or might not ever see Crudley again.

The thought brought a constriction to her throat that

made it impossible to eat. She set down her fork and tried not to feel the emptiness inside that no amount of food could satisfy. She squeezed her eyes shut against the pain. Hot tears coursed down her cheeks. It was too much finally. "Crudley," she said softly. She abandoned herself then to the misery and heard the horrible unfamiliar sound of her own sobbing fill the tiny room. She couldn't even remember the last time she'd cried, and the experience was almost frightening in its intensity, threatening to shatter the walls of self-control she'd so carefully erected for so many years.

The oven timer shrilled loudly. Cass wiped the back of her hand across her eyes and went into the kitchen to take the brownies she'd made for dessert from the oven. She set the pan on a rack to cool and slowly walked back into the main room, heading distractedly for the big bay window overlooking the street.

The window seat was her favorite spot for thinking and dreaming. She could sit for hours watching the barely shifting scene on the peaceful residential street, listening to the small sounds of everyday life. She sat in a corner of the seat and leaned back against the throw pillows, gently moving aside one edge of the sheer draperies to gaze out.

Evening had settled onto the street. Late golden sunlight dripped through the tree leaves, pooling on the sidewalks. In the distance a dog barked and children at play called to one another. The whole scene was so pleasing and familiar that Cass should have felt comforted. Yet it was disconcerting to look out on a world apparently unchanged by any of the tumultuous emotions that tormented her.

For a few moments she didn't even notice the strange car parked across the street and slightly north of her address. Belatedly her attention fixed on the nondescript midsize vehicle whose lack of distinction was itself distinctive in this neighborhood. The car would pass without notice in most parts of town, but on this street it looked almost aggressively bland.

Cass shifted position to study the car from a different angle and noticed the driver still behind the wheel. Even at a distance something about the inclination of the driver's head and the sharply silhouetted profile looked disquietingly familiar.

Cass stiffened and dropped the drape back into place. It couldn't be. Her weary brain tried to deny it, but she knew the truth. Gabe Preston had followed her home and was watching her, no doubt hoping to catch her in a rendezvous with the rest of her gang of thieves. Her pulse began to throb in her temples. How dare he?

Her first impulse was to dash out of the house and across the street and tell him exactly what she thought of him. She restrained the urge. If she just ignored him, eventually he would go away. Unfortunately she found she couldn't relax at all knowing he was out there spying on her. She looked again. He was still out there. It was ridiculous to feel so exposed, so uncomfortable. He couldn't see through her walls, couldn't hear anything she did. Why did she feel so vulnerable knowing he was out there? More importantly what could she do to make him leave?

She could do what any other honest citizen would do if her house were being watched by a strange man. Cass walked to the phone, picked up the receiver and dialed the police. They'd refused to take a report on her stolen cat, but they couldn't refuse to help her with this. "Hello?" she said to the dispatcher who answered her call. "A strange man is parked in front of my neighbor's house and I don't know if anyone is home there or not.'' She paused, waiting for the inevitable questions. "No, no, he isn't actually doing anything right now, but this is a very quiet neighborhood and strangers don't normally hang around on the streets here."

The mention of her address, plus a few more suggestive comments from Cass elicited the desired response from the police dispatcher. "We'll send a car to check," she said.

Satisfied that the police would soon roust her unwanted spy, Cass returned to the window seat and circumspectly lifted the edge of the curtain. Gabe Preston's car was still there. She sat quietly waiting. Mere minutes later a marked patrol car slowly cruised up and parked behind the beige sedan. Two of Newport's finest exited their police car and strolled up on either side of Gabe Preston's car. One of them leaned down to peer in the driver's window and engage Gabe in conversation.

Their talk lasted only a minute or so. Cass could see the officer closest to her smiling and gesturing broadly. Then he briefly touched the brim of his hat in parting, and the two policemen walked back to their cruiser and drove off. The nondescript beige sedan stayed exactly where it was, Gabe slouched down slightly in the seat with his head cocked to one side.

Cass fought down another wave of anger. That was all the police were going to do? Tell the potential burglar "Have a nice day" and drive off, leaving him to plunder the whole neighborhood at will? She expected better of law enforcement in this area. Wasn't that why she lived here? To reap the benefits of wealth by association?

Of course none of the houses on Cass's street could lay claim to the same magnificence the historic summer cottages possessed. No one who lived here had that kind of affluence. Perhaps Gabe Preston had flashed an ornately engraved identification card from Crosswhite Manor. That would certainly trump any influence a resident of Cass's neighborhood could summon.

She let the curtain fall back into place and turned away from the window in disgust. So that was that. Emilie Crosswhite's head of security could do whatever he pleased. No, Cass corrected herself, Emilie Crosswhite's *godson* could do whatever he pleased.

Cass mulled over the implications of the odd dual relationship between Gabriel Preston and Emilie Crosswhite. The upper classes still took seriously the outmoded honorary titles like "godmother." His family and hers must be very close. No wonder Gabe carried himself with so much authority. No wonder he exuded power and self-assurance. He came from money. He assumed superiority as his birthright. He must have been mortified when Cass assumed he was a common laborer.

But what was he doing *working* for Emilie? He certainly couldn't need the money. Maybe he was bored with the idle life of the rich. Cass threw an exasperated look toward the window. Maybe he liked playing cops and robbers, and his doting godmother indulged him.

In any case, Cass was going to have to deal with him on her own. The police weren't going to help with her problem, which was finding a way to make Gabe go home and stop staking out her house.

Marching across the street and telling him off sounded more appealing by the minute. But at last she realized it would be a mistake. Whether he had acted on Emilie Crosswhite's orders or decided to follow her on his own, Gabe had to be observing her with Emilie's knowledge and approval. He would report whatever he learned to his employer. If Cass annoyed him too much, he might convince Emilie to refuse any further cooperation, cooperation that was necessary for securing Crudley's return. Galling as it was to admit it, Cass needed Gabe's goodwill—or at least his lack of animosity. Cass fumed for several minutes. Like it or not, she concluded, she had to be at least civil to the ever-present Mr. Preston.

She stalked into the kitchen to cut herself a brownie, vexed at the feeling of powerlessness her position provoked. Only after she'd dished out a huge square for herself and poured a glass of milk to go with it did she think of another way to deal with Mr. Gabe Preston. She took a second plate from the cupboard, cut a few more brownies and poured some more milk into another glass. Then she headed out her front door and crossed the street. She would be polite and hospitable, but she would have the satisfaction of rubbing Gabe's nose in the fact that she knew what he was up to.

Gabe saw Cass approaching and he sank down behind the wheel of the car, trying to make himself invisible even though it was clearly too late for that. Cass stopped at the driver's-side window. Gabe turned his head to meet her eyes.

"Hello," she said neutrally. "Isn't this the wrong kind of neighborhood for you to be scouting if you're looking for freelance security work?"

The aroma of fresh brownies rose in the evening air. Condensation began to bead on the glass of cold milk. Gabe considered the offerings she'd brought as he considered his answer. He had no plausible reason to be where he was other than the one she'd guessed, and she doubted he would take the trouble to lie. "I'm watching you," he admitted.

Cass tried to keep her agitated emotions from showing on her face. "And what have you found out so far?"

He shrugged. "Not much. I hope I'm going to find out in a minute how good a cook you are."

Cass handed Gabe the plate and he took it, placing it carefully on the dashboard before breaking off the corner of a brownie and popping it in his mouth. "Very good," he said. "Thank you. It was nice of you to bring me food, especially under the circumstances."

"Maybe I'm hoping to convince you I'm just an ordinary working woman with nothing to hide, so you'll go away and leave me alone. Like most normal innocent people, I find it disconcerting to have someone following me around and spying on me."

"I'm sorry it bothers you," he said. Cass thought he even sounded sincere. "But I have to check you out. I owe it to Emilie not to let anyone take advantage of her. She's very naive in certain ways, and consequently very easily manipulated by clever people with hard-luck stories."

"Do you really believe I fall into that category? Do you really believe I'm manipulating Mrs. Crosswhite with a phony hard-luck story?" Her cheeks flushed with heat and her voice tightened.

Gabe regarded her with a coolly appraising, apparently disinterested gaze. "No," he said gently, "I don't. But then, I'm very easily manipulated by beautiful women with great legs and sad hazel eyes. I can't trust my instincts where you're concerned. Not if I expect to protect Emilie."

He had flustered her again. She was sure he did it on purpose, but knowing that didn't help her figure out how to respond. For long moments she was unable to speak at all. When she did, it was without looking at him. "I don't know what you hope to prove by sitting out here. I'm certainly not going to arrange any meetings with my fellow conspirators now that I've seen you here. For all you know, they were waiting inside for me before I came home and are still there now. Or maybe I'm going to use the phone to make my plans. Parking here for hours accomplishes nothing. You have no way of knowing what I'm really doing."

Out of the corner of her eye, Cass saw Gabe shifting around inside the car. He flipped back a tan windbreaker lying on the passenger seat to reveal what it had been covering. He picked up the long cylindrical microphone and held it out in Cass's direction. "I can find out exactly what you're doing, and I don't have to tap your phone or plant bugs in your apartment to do it. This particular device can pick up the sound of a human voice even through walls two-feet thick."

She'd been annoyed several times that day. She'd been frustrated and exasperated. Now she was truly enraged. She realized she was gripping the milk so hard the glass could shatter. Her voice when she spoke was low, shaking with the effort at control. "You rotten, despicable—"

By all rights, he should have let her continue. He deserved every syllable of abuse she could heap on him. "It isn't turned on," he said quickly, his green eyes begging for a reprieve.

Cass stopped on a rising inflection signaling she had plenty more to say. She looked at the monitoring device suspiciously. Gabe gestured toward the on/off switch, clearly at the "off" position, the battery light an unlit bulb indicating no power flowed through the unit. Cass hesitated, mulling over the various implications of what she'd just discovered. She had no way of knowing how long the instrument had been turned off. Gabe could have deactivated it when he heard her open her front door or saw her walking toward him. He could have done it as he reached over to uncover and show it to her. But why tell her about the contraption at all, unless he hoped to make her nervous?

There were too many unknowns to accurately assess Gabe Preston's motives. Cass was sure of only one thing—Gabe had only barely emerged from the level of protozoan slime. She gave him a look that conveyed that opinion, then wordlessly she dumped the glass of milk into his lap, turned and walked away.

Gabe watched Cass go, admiring her trim figure and shapely legs, even as the cold milk puddled uncomfortably along the backs of his thighs. He didn't blame her for being angry and offended by his surveillance. He wasn't proud of what he had felt compelled to do. The legality of the listening device was iffy—a gray area in these circumstances and under current laws. But the ethics were clearly lousy.

He hadn't been able to bring himself to use it, except to frighten her. And what had that gotten him? Gabe squirmed on the wet car seat and reached for a towel he kept stashed underneath it for emergencies. All in all, he had gotten off lucky. She left the brownies.

Chapter Four

In the privacy of her office the next morning, Cass tried to concentrate on the columns of figures before her. Instead, her attention kept straying to the single perfect yellow rose in the crystal bud vase that occupied one corner of her desk. She slapped down her pencil in disgust and tilted back in her chair, covering her eyes with one hand. It didn't help. Behind her closed lids she still saw the image of the flower, as though it had burned itself into her memory. She sighed and opened her eyes. The peace offering, as she thought of it, was right where she'd left it, every bit as beautiful as when she'd discovered it that morning tucked under the windshield wiper of her car.

No note or explanation had accompanied the rose, but Cass knew who'd left it. Hadn't Gabe Preston been in her mind all last night, intruding on her every waking thought and haunting her uneasy dreams? His car had still been parked on the street when she went to bed, but it was gone this morning. In his place, or so Cass assumed, Gabe had left the rose as a kind of apology.

Or was it more? After last night, it was tempting to indulge in a little romantic daydreaming. It seemed like an eternity since Cass had permitted romance in her life, even in fantasy. Gabe Preston certainly provided more than an adequate supply of raw material to dream about; sun-streaked sandy brown hair, eyes the color of the South Seas and a well-muscled body came all too easily to mind, although Cass hadn't realized quite how strong that initial impression of strength and grace had been.

Inevitably concern for Crudley intruded on her brief sensual reverie. She sighed. The two males in her life at the moment were inextricably bound together in her thoughts, as were the pleasure and pain of thinking about either. Her cat, whom she'd loved and taken care of for more than fifteen years, had been stolen and put in who knew what kind of danger? And the man whose cooperation she desperately needed to secure Crudley's safe return thought she was a crook.

Cass wondered again, with increased irritation, why Gabe Preston was working on his godmother's estate in the kind of position usually held by a retired state trooper. A little law-enforcement experience and the ability to wield power discreetly were all the head of estate security really required. Gabriel Preston doubtless substituted his familiarity with all Emilie Crosswhite's friends and the knack of looking terrific in a tuxedo, but what could he possibly know about investigating *her?*

More importantly what could he possibly know about solving Crudley's kidnapping? Cass would have been better off dealing with a professional—someone who knew what he was doing and would use Emilie's social position to coerce the local authorities into helping out if necessary. Gabe Preston was so blindly sure of himself and so impressed with his high-tech espionage toys that he would never admit to being out of his depth. Cass wished he'd stuck to digging a moat around Crosswhite Manor or whatever it was he'd been doing the first time she saw him.

She glanced at the clock. The minutes were creeping by. Now that she knew the police would not help her, the delay in recovering Crudley seemed both pointless and aggravating. If she had some way to contact the kidnappers, she would change the plan and give them the money that very day. The longer they had Crudley, the more chance there was that they would discover their error. Even a child could tell a boy cat from a girl cat if he looked closely enough. And if the kidnappers found out they'd snatched the wrong cat, would they try to brazen it out and hold Crudley for ransom, anyway? Or would they smell a trap and just dump him as fast as they could, out in the woods or on some busy city street where he'd be lost to Cass for all time?

A knock on the door interrupted Cass's dreary speculations. Annie, her secretary, poked her head into the office. "I'm going to lunch now, Cass. Can I bring you anything?"

Cass shook her head and smiled distractedly. "No thanks, Annie."

Annie nodded and started to close the door, then stopped. "Is everything all right?" she asked. Her warm eyes clouded with concern.

Cass tried to put more voltage into her smile. "Everything's fine. Thanks for asking, though."

Annie pressed her lips together into a tight line, a sign she didn't believe a word. After a moment she withdrew.

Cass stared at the closed door and wished she felt able to talk to Annie about her problems. But she'd allowed concern for petty office protocol to limit a potential friendship.

She sighed and tried to focus on the columns of numbers neatly arrayed across the sheets of computer printout. The afternoon dragged on as slowly as the morning. By the time she headed home in the late-August heat, she had a throbbing headache. Neither her mood nor her pain were improved by the appearance, shortly after her arrival home, of the nondescript beige sedan from which Gabe Preston had staked out her house the day before.

Even though she'd half expected it, had almost been watching for it, the renewed surveillance chafed her. She hadn't forgiven Gabe for suspecting her of some as yet unspecified wrongdoing, although clearly his distrustful feelings toward her were ambivalent. He'd brought along a lot of high-tech equipment to spy on her, but then apparently decided not to use it. When confronted he'd admitted straight out what he was doing and why, instead of lying or equivocating. And despite the fact that she'd dumped a glass of milk in his lap, he'd left a rose for her as a kind of reparation.

Remembering her rash behavior the night before brought an embarrassed flush to her cheeks. She'd gone out to face Gabe with every intention of being pleasant. Instead, she'd let him goad her into acting like a child. For a moment's satisfaction, spurred by an unreasoning anger, she'd jeopardized Crudley's safety. Viewed from that angle, Gabe's continued surveillance was a comfort. It meant he hadn't given up all thought of allowing Emilie Crosswhite to help her. For that, she was grateful. For that, she should make an effort—a more successful effort—to be gracious to the annoying Mr. Preston.

Cass finished chopping the vegetables for the pasta primavera she planned for dinner. While the vegetables steamed, the sauce simmered and the water for the pasta heated, Cass took a bottle of chilled white wine from the refrigerator. She opened it expertly and poured a small amount into a wineglass. Holding it up to admire the clear pale color of the Riesling, she made a little toast to herself and took a sip. She closed her eyes and pictured a serene summer evening spent on a riverbank. For a moment, the fantasy was almost palpable. Sighing, Cass allowed the aromas of dinner and the soft whir of the air conditioner to bring her back to the present.

She took one final peek out the window facing the street. The beige sedan was parked in the same place as when she'd last looked. She poured a second glass of wine and headed out to confront Gabe Preston.

He was slouched comfortably behind the wheel of his car, affecting a casual attitude toward his surveillance. Nonetheless, Cass felt the intensity of his observation as she walked toward him. She wished she hadn't changed out of her work clothes. Her white shorts suddenly felt far too short, her azure tank top far too revealing regardless of the heat that made the outfit completely practical. She reminded herself that Gabe only made personal comments to perturb her, and tonight she intended to be fully in control.

She reached the car and held out the glass of wine, in Gabe's direction, carefully keeping it outside the open window. "Dinner is ready," she said matter-of-factly, as though he'd been waiting to be called. "Do you want to come in or shall I bring it out?"

Gabe appeared to consider the offer. "I don't know," he said, "I'm not really dressed for dinner." He gestured vaguely at his T-shirt and shorts. Cass looked puzzled. "I'm not wearing waterproof pants," he clarified.

Unwanted color invaded Cass's cheeks and she dropped

her gaze to the pavement. "You know more about your own table manners than I do," she said touchily. Biting her lip, she tried for a more conciliatory response. "You don't have to worry about me, though, if that's what you mean."

"That's what I mean."

Cass raised her eyes to meet his, forcing herself to do the difficult but correct thing. "Look, I'm sorry, okay? I've had a few really terrible days. I thought losing Crudley was the final straw. Then you showed up with that ridiculous high-powered espionage equipment and I, well, I just snapped."

The corners of Gabe's mouth twitched in amusement. "Your gracious apology is accepted," he said ironically. "I assume you've already accepted mine?"

"The rose?" Cass ventured. Gabe nodded. She felt outmaneuvered again. "It's beautiful," she conceded. "Thank you."

"So we have a truce?"

Cass proffered the wine again and stepped back, leaving Gabe lots of room to open his car door. "We have a truce," she agreed.

"Then lead on. I'm starved."

The coolness of her carriage house came as a welcome relief, even though she had spent very few minutes outside. She could imagine how good it would feel to a man who'd been keeping vigil in a hot car. "Have a seat," Cass instructed, "while I finish up in the kitchen."

"Thanks. Mind if I look around a bit first?" Gabe tried to make the request sound offhand. In truth he was naturally curious about the woman who'd invited him to dinner. But he saw Cass's back stiffen and her hands clench, and he knew she understood his other purpose for asking even before she answered.

"Suit yourself. You won't find any of my co-conspirators hiding in the closets. Or any magazines with the letters cut out."

Gabe sighed inwardly, wondering what had happened to his fabled subtle investigative technique. Admittedly he hadn't made much effort to conceal his suspicions from Cass, but everything he said or did seemed to set her off. She acted like he was the enemy. He ran a hand through his hair and sighed audibly this time. She acted like any worried stressed-out innocent person would act under the circumstances. He stepped quickly into her bedroom, hoping to avoid any further verbal wrangling.

The room surprised him. A big brass bed covered with a handmade quilt dominated the far wall, gleaming softly in the late sunlight filtering through the shades. A brass-and-glass table holding a phone and a lamp stood next to the bed. A cherry chest of drawers, two bookcases and a rocker completed the furnishings.

The paintings, however, quickly drew Gabe's complete attention. The first one he approached was a watercolor. From a distance it resembled a page from an atlas, with a color-coded key in the lower left corner, a stylized directional compass just above the key and the depiction of an unfamiliar island filling the central space. On closer inspection, the picture was clearly a work of fantasy. The colors of the sea and land seemed to swirl and blend into each other, blurring their borderlines at some places, creating impossible boundaries at others. And along one edge a tiny sea serpent seemed to curl around a misty rock—until you blinked or shifted position, and then you saw only a barren outcropping. The place-names were unreadable, written in a language that looked like a cross between Gaelic and Arabic. The words themselves were a kind of abstract art form, visually appealing, hauntingly evocative, and yet without any precise meaning he could put his finger on. Worked into the design along the bottom right-hand edge was the only recognizable English word on the whole painting—the signature of the artist, "Appleton."

Gabe dragged his attention away from the painting reluctantly. He wasn't here to admire Cass's work. It was of interest only insofar as it revealed the kind of woman she was.

He moved on to the bookshelves. They held a variety of ceramic and glass objects, most of them variations of miniature houses. Pottery cottages, homey- and cozy-looking, squatted humbly or rose several stories with tiny turrets and dormers jutting out at odd angles. Each one had a tiny cat sunning on the front mat, gazing out a window or climbing a trellis. Gabe knew, without having to search for her signature or mark, that Cass had made these, too.

Despite his resolve to remain detached, Gabe had to admire Cass's talent. But her viewpoint troubled him. Maps of imaginary places. Landscapes without human perspective. Houses where no one lived. It was the vision of a loner—a woman who'd insulated herself from personal contact with others and deliberately chosen to walk a solitary path.

A woman like that might have no compunction about taking advantage of other people. They simply wouldn't matter in her private world. A woman like that would say or do anything to get what she wanted, letting other people suffer the consequences of her selfishness. A woman like that—

Gabe stopped himself. Cass wasn't "a woman like that," at least not on the basis of what he'd uncovered so far. He had to stick to the facts and let them speak for themselves.

At the moment all he knew was that Cass Appleton was a hardworking headstrong woman caught up in circumstances beyond her control. She had forced herself to overcome her natural shyness to try to save her cat, but she wasn't comfortable asking anyone for help. He had no reason to condemn her, even though he had no reason to trust her completely, either.

So, lighten up, Preston, he admonished himself. She isn't going to confess because you intimidate her. She's too strong to break and too feisty to bend. She'll only fight back. So relax and try to be charming. This isn't the worst duty you've ever pulled.

When he wandered back into the living room, he found Cass loudly and overly ambitiously setting the table. "Find anything interesting?" she asked in a tight angry voice.

Gabe surveyed the living room walls and saw more watercolors: landscapes of lush rolling hills and ethereal cliffs and mountains, all done in a kind of misty otherworldly style he now thought of as distinctly Cass Appleton's. "You're very talented," he said.

Cass brought her head up with a jerk and stared at Gabe. She hadn't expected him to notice the art. She'd assumed he'd be checking under her bed and inside her closets for clues. His praise left her speechless.

"It's an unusual combination," Gabe continued. He drew closer to a painting in shades of black and gray that was oddly luminous when it should have been somber. "An artist and a CPA."

Cass made herself release the death grip she had on the silverware. "I see you've done your homework," she said through clenched teeth.

"I told you I was going to check up on you. It wasn't very difficult to find out where you work."

"Are you bugging my office, too?"

Gabe walked into the tiny kitchen/dining area where Cass stood frozen in anger. Placing his hands gently on her rigid shoulders, he turned her to face him. She refused to meet his eyes. "No," he said softly, "I am not bugging your office. Or your house. And I'm doing a damn lousy job of investigating you, mostly because I can't find it in me to believe you would be involved in a plan to hurt Emilie, especially now that you've met her."

"Then why don't you just leave me alone?" Cass's voice combined defiance with plaintiveness in a way that made her feel about ten years old.

"I can't do that. For two reasons. First, I have a responsibility to protect Emilie. I know a mentally competent adult should be able to take care of herself, but Emilie Crosswhite is a special case. Over fifty years ago she married a man who adored her and treated her like a hothouse flower to be shielded from all the harsh realities of life most people take for granted. I doubt she's ever read a newspaper or watched the nightly news on television. She gets her information from the women she plays bridge with or from what she overhears at social functions. She's not completely ignorant of world events, but for five decades such things had no meaning for her or her life. Hartley Crosswhite wanted it that way, and Emilie was an old-fashioned wife, devoted to her husband, willing to cater to his every whim and ask no questions."

Gabe paused, but when Cass made no response, he continued. "Hartley's death two years ago destroyed Emilie's familiar cozy existence. At first she was completely lost. Now, to her credit, she's trying hard to learn what she missed all those years. She has a strong humanitarian streak, but no ability to discriminate or judge between the legitimate causes and the scams. She's filled the estate payroll with recent immigrants and political refugees from half the impoverished nations of the world. For a while, if you didn't speak at least ten languages, you couldn't even coax a cup of coffee from the staff."

Gabe put a hand under Cass's chin and tilted her head up, compelling her to look at him. "The point I'm trying to make is, I have a certain responsibility to safeguard Emilie Crosswhite, from herself as much as from outsiders. When I accepted that responsibility, I accepted everything that goes with it—all the inconvenience, the unpleasant duties, all the frustration and pain you expose yourself to when you choose to make yourself accountable for what happens to someone else. Do you understand?"

Gabe would probably scoff at the comparison, but Cass felt exactly that way about Crudley. She was the cat's guardian, his caretaker, as well as his friend. "I understand," she said softly. "What's the second reason?"

"What?"

"You said there were two reasons you wouldn't leave me alone. What's the second one?"

Cass looked up into Gabe's sea green eyes, shadowed by dark lashes. His expression was suddenly intimate. Cass caught her breath. "It's that I think," he said, "*you* are going to need my help, too—whether you're one of the good guys or one of the bad."

Illogically, Cass had foreseen a different revelation. She pulled away from Gabe and folded her arms defensively across her breasts. Her emotional barricade was firmly back in place. "You're wrong," she said, choosing to ignore Gabe's clearly articulated doubts about her character. "I don't need your help. Once Mrs. Crosswhite tells me when and where to leave the ransom, I can get my cat back on my own. I won't need any further assistance from you or anyone else."

Shaking his head almost imperceptibly, Gabe forced a crooked smile. "I hope, for your sake, that you're wrong." He sidestepped past her into the kitchen and lifted the lid off a pot to sniff the sauce she'd prepared.

Cass spun around to confront him. "I hate those cryptic comments you're always making. What is that one supposed to mean?"

Gabe replaced the lid and met her irritated gaze with a coolly level one. "It means I don't think being able to claim you never need anyone else's help should necessarily be the highest aspiration in life. *Dependence* may be a dirty word in your book, but personally I don't see anything wrong with people offering a little support and comfort to others, or taking it, either."

Cass raised one eyebrow loftily. "I don't imagine *you* would see anything wrong with it."

"Now it's my turn. What is that comment supposed to mean?"

"It means I'm tired of being judged by someone who couldn't possibly understand my situation or my problems. You've obviously never been dependent in your life. You've never had to worry about whether there will be food on the table or a roof over your head. Everything you've ever needed or wanted has been handed to you because of the simple fact you were born into the right family."

Hot blood rose to Cass's cheeks as days of frustration found an outlet and a target. "You think dependence is a desirable quality? It's easy enough to achieve. Give away all your money, quit playing security guard for your godmother and get a real job—the kind where you can be laid off, downsized or fired at any time. Then maybe you'll realize dependency isn't a choice for most people, and obligation isn't a luxury they can choose to accept or not. They're facts of life.''

"I guess I thought that was my point," Gabe said quietly.

They stared at each other for long moments. Cass's temper cooled quickly after the uncharacteristic outburst, replaced by shame that she'd permitted this stranger to see the darker side of her heart. "I promised you a truce," she mumbled, fussing with the table settings.

"We still have one, at least as far as I'm concerned."

He was letting her off the hook. Cass took a deep breath and nodded her silent concurrence to the renewed cease-fire. She walked to the stove. Somehow she had dodged disaster again.

As she drained the pasta, Cass mentally berated herself. She could not count on Gabe Preston continuing to overlook her barbed remarks. For Crudley's sake, she had to stop being so touchy, no matter how much the man annoyed her. He was nobody important in the larger scheme of things. Once she had Crudley back, he would disappear from her life, as so many other brief acquaintances had, vanishing into the nameless faceless void of soon-forgotten memories.

Looking up, Cass found Gabe watching her with his sea green eyes, a mysterious half smile curving his lips. Her stomach fluttered—from hunger, no doubt—as she turned away from his disquieting scrutiny to serve dinner.

She set down the plates while Gabe gallantly held out her chair for her, waiting to seat her at her own kitchen table as though she was dining at an elegant restaurant. The courtliness of the gesture suffused her with pleasure, even though she half suspected Gabe meant it as a joke. His expression denied any trickery, though, and Cass began to understand how Emilie Crosswhite could be so smitten with her godson. As she picked up her fork and toyed with her food, Cass wondered how easily, in fact, Gabe Preston's memory would vanish once this kidnapping ordeal was ended.

Chapter Five

The next evening when Cass arrived home, she saw Gabe Preston's beige sedan parked in front of her house. The man himself, however, was noticeably missing. A feeling like disappointment swept over her. She'd expected Gabe to be waiting. True, she'd been late leaving her office. Her inability to concentrate the past few days had seriously disrupted her work schedule. She had to stay an extra hour just to keep from falling behind at her job. But she hadn't thought Gabe would give up so quickly and go wandering around the neighborhood looking for more excitement just because he couldn't spy on her.

Perhaps it wasn't really fair to say he'd been spying on her, Cass admitted as she walked up the tree-shaded path to the carriage house. A spy was supposed to be furtive, not straightforward and candid, as Gabe had been. A spy should sneak around secretly and lurk in the bushes, not eat dinner with his quarry and then stay around until almost midnight telling stories and playing gin rummy. Gabe had done that and more to entertain her last night, disguising the real purpose of his surveillance so well that their time together had seemed almost like a date. His absence now felt almost like a rejection.

Cass shook off that ridiculous notion as she climbed the stairs to her door. Before she could insert the key in the lock, she heard soft music coming from inside her apartment. She pushed on the door and discovered it was already open. Suddenly Gabe Preston's whereabouts were no longer a mystery.

He was chopping vegetables in her kitchen, tossing them into her big wooden salad bowl. When he heard the front door slam, he glanced up and smiled broadly. The look on her face should have dropped him in his tracks, but it didn't seem to faze him at all. "You're late," he said cheerfully.

"I can see that," Cass answered through gritted teeth.

Gabe put down his knife, *her* knife, and added some guilt to his expression. "Look, I know how this must seem to you. A man who's practically a stranger barges into your home when you're not here—"

"Breaks in," Cass corrected angrily. All her good feelings vanished under a tide of anger and indignation. Her privacy had been violated inexcusably.

"All right, 'breaks in,' if you like. I won't argue semantics right now. You shouldn't leave a key under your mat like that, though. It's the first place a burglar would look. Your insurance company could give you a hard time if you had to file a claim. In this instance it worked out to your benefit since I'd brought all this food to prepare dinner. When you didn't come home when you should have, I sat in a sweltering car with my steaks threatening to go bad and the wine heating up and the flowers wilting, and I knew you wouldn't want everything to spoil. I did try to call you, but your switchboard quits at five..."

"So you broke in."

Gabe took a deep breath. "I guess you could say that."

"There isn't any other way to say it. Get out. Now."

Gabe walked around the counter and moved toward Cass. She dodged him and crossed rapidly to the bedroom, intending to slam the door in his face if he followed. He caught her before she could reach its sanctuary and grabbed one of her wrists to slow her progress.

"Wait a minute. Wait a minute!" He spun Cass around and grasped her shoulders. "Everything you've said is legitimate, and everything you're feeling is justified. But listen to me for a minute. What if things were just a little bit different from the way you're seeing them? What if you and I were friends, and we'd made plans to have dinner together and then you were unavoidably delayed? Would you want me to sit and wait outside in an overheated car, or would you want me to let myself in if I knew where you kept a spare key? And if I started dinner for you because I knew you'd be hot and tired when you finally did come home, wouldn't you be happy, not angry, that I'd come in and started without you?"

"But we're not friends," Cass reminded him.

"Aren't we? I thought we made some pretty strong progress in that direction last night. You relaxed, I relaxed, we had a pleasant dinner and a nice evening together. That sounds friendly to me."

"It was purely professional. You're watching me because you're trying to catch me doing something suspicious. You think I'm a crook."

Gabe ran his hands lightly down Cass's upper arms, sending a chill through her in the air-conditioned room. "It doesn't matter what I think. I've tried to explain that to you. Where Emilie Crosswhite's welfare is concerned, I have to suspend my own beliefs and remain skeptical of anyone who could hurt her. For better or worse, that description fits you at the moment. Emilie likes you. And she's a sucker for a hard-luck story, especially if it involves children or small furry animals. She wants to help you. *I* want to help you. But that doesn't mean I can disregard using common sense or ignore the reasonable doubts anyone would have about your story. I have to protect Emilie."

Cass pushed away from him. "But *I'm* the victim. Not Mrs. Crosswhite. Not you. Me. It's my cat that was stolen and it's my money that's going to buy him back. No one is being taken advantage of but me. None of what has happened is my fault. I didn't do anything to deserve this kind of punishment, but I'm being punished, anyway, and for no reason other than I wanted the best care I could find for my cat when I went out of town."

Gabe reached for her, but Cass flinched away. "I know this has been rough on you," he began.

"Rough?" Cass repeated, fighting to keep the bitterness from her voice. "You don't have the slightest idea how I feel. My cat has been kidnapped. It's going to cost every cent I have in the world to save him. I've been forced to ask a complete stranger for one small favor, and for that I've been labeled a crook and been spied on and had my apartment broken into. Yes, I guess you could say the last few days have been rough."

"Maybe," Gabe suggested softly, "that's all the more reason for you to try and stop thinking of me as the enemy and start thinking of me as your friend. Emilie isn't the only one with a weakness for hard-luck stories. A damsel in distress, especially a damsel with big hazel eyes, gorgeous legs and the ability to leap tall fences in almost a single bound, can make my knees weaken every time."

Gabe reached for her again, and this time Cass didn't

push him away. Rigidly she endured being enfolded in his arms, unconsciously nestling her head against his shoulder. Gabe's big lightly calloused hand stroked her hair. She fought the temptation to simply yield completely to the sense of security and protection stealing over her, fought the irrational belief that somehow this man would see to it that everything worked out all right for her and Crudley.

"I'm truly sorry I've upset you. I should have guessed how you'd react to this kind of intrusion, no matter how good my intentions were. I was so caught up in my plans to make dinner for you tonight, I forgot you didn't even know about them. I figured you knew I'd be here, and after last night I assumed you wouldn't let me sit out there in a hot car all those hours. So I skipped a few admittedly crucial steps and went right to what I thought the outcome would be, anyway. I guess I figured what I planned to do was a lot less obnoxious than most of what I'd already done to you in the last two days. Not much of an excuse, I know, but it's the truth."

Cass wanted to stay angry with Gabe. He had earned her anger, and worse. But wrapped in the shelter of his arms, feeling the slow steady beat of his heart against her cheek, she felt her hostility dissolving like morning mist burned off by the sun. After all, he'd meant well. Only make the one small change in interpretation, only say that they really were friends, and nothing he'd done would have been out of line.

"I went directly to the kitchen and stayed there," Gabe added, as if countering more of her unvoiced objections. "I didn't search anywhere or look around at anything, not even the paintings and ceramics, even though I really wanted to see all of them again."

In spite of her resolve not to forgive Gabe just yet,

Cass's indignation diminished further. Her art nurtured an important if recently neglected facet of her identity. She was surprised and pleased that Gabe had not only noticed her work but liked it. "Well," she said, softening, "if the dinner is any good, maybe I'll take you on a guided tour later."

"That would be nice," Gabe murmured. "I can't imagine any better way to travel through imaginary lands than with the person who created them." He released her with apparent reluctance. "Right now, though, I'd better finish making the salad and then throw the steaks under the broiler or we'll never eat." He turned and walked back to the kitchen.

Cass went into the bedroom, emerging a short time later in a coral T-shirt and faded cutoffs, her hair twisted up and caught with a barrette. When he saw her, Gabe smiled broadly. "Ah," he said, "the real Cass Appleton."

Cass pushed a stray tendril of her dark hair behind one ear and grimaced. "I'm just a peasant at heart," she said with forced lightness.

"You aren't a gray pinstripe-suited CPA at heart, that's for sure. How did you wind up working for Laughlin and Denmore as an accountant?"

"I had to make a living," Cass said shortly.

"Couldn't you have found something that makes better use of your natural gifts? I'm sure you're a fine CPA, but this—" he gestured toward the paintings on the walls "—is obviously what you love."

"I also love eating and having a roof over my head."

"Not all artists starve. Quite a few make a living using their talent in some way. Musicians tune pianos or give private lessons to supplement their income. You could teach or work in a frame shop or an art-supply house.

There are plenty of jobs that would keep you closer to what you love to do."

Cass reached into the salad bowl and snitched a piece of carrot, avoiding Gabe's clear-eyed gaze. "I suppose I could scratch out a living doing what you're talking about—hanging around the fringes of the art world and occasionally using a bit of my skill in that area. But I don't want to exist like that, hand-to-mouth, always wondering where the next month's rent will come from, always worrying about whether I have the money to buy supplies to do any paintings or ceramics. That kind of stress over a long period of time kills off any creative urges, I guarantee you. It isn't true, at least in my case, that suffering produces great art."

"Being a CPA, at least in your case, isn't producing any art at all," Gabe observed. "Everything I've seen here was done at least two years ago. Where's the work in progress? What have you done since you started working for Laughlin and Denmore?"

One part of Cass's mind urged her to lash out at Gabe and tell him it was none of his business. The prevailing part—the part that prompted almost daily feelings of guilt and dissatisfaction—agreed with Gabe's assessment and his implied criticism. "Life isn't that simple," she said lamely. "I've been extremely busy since I joined the firm. I'm the junior associate and the only woman they've ever hired. I have to be twice as good as anyone else just to be considered equal."

"I'm sure it's been difficult. My question is why you're subjecting yourself to that in the first place. If it was something you really wanted, really cared about, it would be worth any struggle and hardship to do. But you hate it."

Cass's head jerked up and she looked at Gabe with

startled, almost frightened intensity. "I don't hate it," she insisted.

"Maybe *hate* is too strong a word," Gabe conceded. "But it's certainly making you unhappy."

Cass didn't bother to deny it. "A lot of things make me unhappy, including having my cat stolen and my place broken into. It hasn't exactly been a great week. That doesn't mean I'm ready to throw away my whole career and go live on roots and berries in the woods."

Gabe shook his head. "The next forty years is a long time to spend doing work that gives you no satisfaction. Is money so important that you would sacrifice anything for it?"

"Not money for its own sake. I know you can't relate to this, but most people want the same things I want—a home of their own, a family, someone to love them—and they know that they can't have those things until they achieve a certain level of financial security."

"No one will love you unless you're rich?"

"I can't allow myself to fall in love with anyone until I'm in the right financial position to."

"I didn't know that was something you could control."

"It's easy enough to stay out of love," Cass said wryly. "A little dose of reality is all it takes to kill most fantasies."

"I'm not sure I agree. Some dreams die harder than others. Some refuse to die at all."

The conversation had become dangerously personal and taken on undercurrents Cass couldn't define. The chance she could nudge Gabe Preston into disclosing something that would give her an advantage over him was more than matched by the possibility she would say something he considered incriminating. Hadn't he been trying to make her relax, talking about her art, pretending concern for her job dissatisfaction, most likely hoping to lull her into dropping her guard and revealing information that would implicate her in the extortion plan?

Cass tried to shift the conversation without being too obvious. "Well, you're lucky not to have to worry about finances. You can do whatever you like, whenever you like. You can choose to have a job or not and never worry about the pay."

"I am a fortunate man," Gabe agreed with a slight bitterness Cass found puzzling.

"It must be nice working for Emilie Crosswhite. She seems like a sweet person. She certainly seems to dote on you."

"Emilie is the best. If she hadn't given me the job on her estate, I'm not sure what I would have done with myself."

The intensity and utter sincerity of Gabe's last statement forced Cass to reconsider some of her opinions. "You really take your work seriously, don't you?"

"Of course I do." Gabe looked amazed that Cass might have doubted it. "You of all people should know exactly how seriously I take it."

Cass shrugged and avoided Gabe's too-direct gaze. "I suppose I thought you enjoyed playing at having a job."

"Sorry to disappoint you. Being Emilie Crosswhite's chief of security isn't the only job I've ever held or the only job I've ever loved. But it's an important job, I'm good at it, and I'm grateful Emilie hired me. Does that give me a little credibility with you? My advice may be free, but it isn't totally worthless."

"I never said it was." Cass turned away from him and opened the refrigerator, searching for the salad dressing. "I only said that I put a lot of thought into choosing a profession and invested a lot of time and money training to be the best at it I could be."

"I could spend a lot of time and money training to become a jockey," Gabe countered, "and when I was through, I would still be a foot too tall and eighty pounds too heavy to ride racehorses and win. You can't force yourself to become something you're not suited for, either emotionally or physically. The costs are too high."

Cass raised one eyebrow. "So you finally gave up trying to be a jockey and became Emilie Crosswhite's chief of security, instead?"

Gabe threw up his hands in surrender. "You win. I'll stop preaching, at least until after dinner."

"Make it an all-night cease-fire," Cass suggested, "or I'll have indigestion just thinking about you starting up again."

"You've got a deal. And now, since you can't stand the heat, get out of the kitchen and I'll finish the steaks. You could open the wine in the meantime. I really liked what we had last night, so I brought a bottle of the same thing."

Cass stared at him incredulously. "You brought your own wine?"

"Hey! I'm not a complete deadbeat. When I take a lady to dinner in her own apartment, I do it right."

Cass found the wine lying on the bottom shelf of the refrigerator. "I can see that now," she said. "What did you fix for dessert?"

Gabe looked crestfallen. "Are all those wonderful brownies gone?"

"As a matter of fact, they're not."

"Good. I mean, that's what I thought. I didn't want them to go to waste. I'll make dessert next time—not that it will be nearly as good as yours."

Next time? Cass fumbled with the corkscrew. Was Gabe Preston planning to take up residence on her doorstep and in her kitchen for the duration of the kidnapping ordeal? The prospect wasn't nearly as awful as it should have been.

Cass had grown used to her chosen solitude and rarely felt lonely anymore. But she suspected the past few days would have been even more miserable without Gabe Preston's alternately pleasing and irritating presence. It had kept her from dwelling too much on Crudley's plight or spending useless hours of misery contemplating her helplessness. The man was good company. There was no denying that.

Cass poured the wine and cautioned herself not to become too enthralled by the magnetic Mr. Preston. Charm was his stock-in-trade. It was probably his primary qualification for the job at Emilie Crosswhite's estate. He wasn't lazy and he'd thought about his life—Cass had to grant him that. But they had absolutely nothing in common beyond the temporary artificial link created by Crudley's kidnapping. Once her cat was home safely and Gabe had fulfilled his duty to protect his godmother and employer, he would be gone forever.

In the meantime, however, there was no reason she shouldn't enjoy Gabe's companionship. She was stuck with him, regardless, so she might as well make the best of it. She handed him a glass of wine and smiled into his beautiful eyes. He lightly touched the rim of his glass to hers. "To Crudley," he said, "and his return."

Cass's newfound resolve to go with the flow of events that had been imposed on her lasted throughout dinner. The steak was delicious, tender and juicy, marinated with a sauce Gabe claimed was an old Preston-family secret.

He served the food, refilled her wineglass and regaled her with funny stories.

After they'd finished eating, Gabe asked for a guided tour of her artwork. Blushing with barely concealed pleasure, Cass walked with him to the bedroom. Gabe went immediately to Cass's own favorite of her paintings, the imaginary map hung on the wall opposite the bed where she could see it every night before sleeping. He stared at it for a long time without speaking.

"It's wonderful," he said. "It makes me want to go there and I don't even know where it is."

Cass laughed lightly. "It isn't anywhere—except in my mind. It's a place I made up."

"But you've made it seem real—more real than most of the countries we hear about in the news and can't even imagine except as a shadowy imitation of our own. This has a kind of substance. It makes you feel like you know exactly the kind of people who must live there, even though they're nothing like anyone else you know."

His insight into her creative process sent a chill down Cass's spine. No one had ever put into words so clearly what she'd been trying to do in her painting. Her work had never lacked admirers among the few she showed it to, but understanding came infrequently, if ever.

"Who does live there?" Gabe asked her, so softly she barely heard him at first. "Where are all the people?"

A warning bell sounded deep inside Cass. She stepped away from the painting, over to the shelves, automatically picking up one of the small houses and running her fingers over its reassuring contours.

"There are no people in any of your work," Gabe said, pressing his point. "Maps, landscapes and houses with animals as their only occupants. Where are all the people?"

"I was never particularly interested in portraiture," Cass hedged.

"Is that why you don't have any photographs anywhere?"

Cass looked up in alarm, her trepidation growing. She should never have agreed to let Gabe see her work again. He was too observant. Worse, he was too accurate in his analysis of what he noted. "I know what reality looks like," she said quietly. "I don't need pictures to remind me."

"Not even of Crudley?"

So that was what had sparked his curiosity. A jumble of emotions swept through her. She should have experienced only relief at having the conversation veer from the area of the painfully personal back to the safer ground of neutrally professional inquiry. Instead, she felt a stab of distress. Gabe still considered her a suspect in the extortion scheme, still apparently didn't believe she really owned a cat named Crudley. Most of all, Cass noticed the unexpected regret flooding her heart as Gabe's question instantly resurrected the barriers between them, closing off the growing intimacy they seemed to have shared only moments before.

"There are pictures of Crudley," she said, replacing the pottery house on its shelf. She turned to face Gabe. "In an album, though, not framed and hanging on the walls. I'm not an idiot, Mr. Preston," she added. "And I'm not a six-year-old playing games or a frustrated spinster sublimating her maternal urges by keeping a pet. I don't dress my cat up in cute clothes or talk baby talk to him. He's a cat. Not a toy. Not a person. A cat. That's all."

"A cat you're willing to pay ten thousand dollars to have back."

"I suppose it's impossible for you to understand why someone would do that."

"Not necessarily. Why don't you explain it to me?"

Cass stood silently with her arms folded across her breasts. How much, if anything, should she confess to this man? He still had the power to deny her Emilie Crosswhite's assistance. But beyond the undeniable logic of offering Gabe some explanation for her actions, Cass felt an almost overwhelming urge to confide in him, as though he alone might be capable of understanding and empathizing with what compelled her to act as she had. Something in his eyes, in his manner, invited her trust. She longed for the closeness she'd felt with him earlier.

She studied the imaginary map, counting on it to calm her as she made the decision to speak. "The rest of the photographs you won't find hanging on the wall are snapshots of my family. We didn't own a camera, so there aren't many pictures of our little group. It's an ever-changing cast, however. My mother married four times. She believed in the institution of marriage, but she didn't have very good taste in men. Attractive charming bums were her downfall. Neither my father nor any of my stepfathers seemed to be able to find or hold a steady job. My mother was our sole support most of the time. We moved a lot, one step ahead of the creditors."

Cass risked a quick look at Gabe. His eyes were fixed on her, his expression encouraging her to continue. "One day, our most recent neighbors moved out. They didn't want to take their children's pets with them. My stepfather put his foot down about letting me have the dog, but the four-month-old kitten looked like little enough trouble. He already had the name 'Crudley.' I don't know why. But after he became my cat, the constant turmoil of my life stopped mattering so much. Houses and apartments came and went, stepfathers came and went, schools and friends came and went, but every night when I curled up to sleep, I had Crudley. He stayed and he loved me—at least I believed he did, despite whatever else changed.''

Cass had thought about her attachment to Crudley a hundred times, but had never really explained it to another person. She wondered how it must sound to someone who'd lived through a completely different type of childhood or who had found other ways to cope with adolescent traumas. As she waited for Gabe's reaction, Cass kept her eyes on the watercolor of the illusory island where everyone lived happily ever after.

Gabe took a step forward, put his arms around Cass and pulled her close. "We'll get Crudley back," he whispered against her hair. "I promise you that." Gabe spoke without thinking, not considering the implications of his remark until the words were already out of his mouth. Just as quickly, he regretted his automatic response to Cass. Hadn't he as much as said he believed her story? Wasn't that the same as admitting he believed in her? How could he have allowed his carefully cultivated skepticism to melt away the first time Cass revealed even a hint of vulnerability?

Gabe knew he should say something to clarify his comment, for both their sakes. He needed to correct any misimpression he might have given Cass that she was no longer under suspicion. But the warm scent of her skin clouded his thoughts. Her silken hair brushed softly against his cheek. And despite her rigid posture and her resistance to being comforted, Cass fit against his body as though she belonged there.

With a tiny sigh Gabe felt more than heard, Cass yielded slightly in his arms. The small but significant surrender sent a surge of protectiveness through Gabe. He fought the instinct, as he had been fighting most of his instincts since he met Cass. He could not afford to trust her. He could not afford to be wrong about her. His arms tightened around Cass as if he, not she, were the one who needed the emotional support and physical warmth of their embrace. He closed his eyes, and for a few long moments permitted himself to forget everything except how good it felt to hold her.

Reluctantly, Gabe forced himself to release Cass. "I'd better go," he said, the huskiness of his voice betraying emotions best left unexamined.

"Already?" Cass's cheeks were pink and her eyes sparked with unshed tears. She bit her lower lip and turned away from Gabe. "I mean, you haven't had your dessert yet," she said over her shoulder as she left him alone in the bedroom.

Gabe could imagine what it cost Cass to ask him to stay, even a little longer. It would be cruel to reject her overture and abandon her when she had made the effort to reach out to him. He would just have to control his own emotions. Taking a deep breath, he strolled into the kitchen where Cass was concentrating far too intently on cutting up brownies and scooping up ice cream to go with them.

"Now that I think about it," he said casually, "my schedule tonight is pretty flexible." He grinned wryly. "Actually, there's a John Wayne film festival on television. I was going to catch one of the Westerns later, but it won't kill me to miss it. I've seen most of them a dozen times already."

Cass gave up the pretense of being absorbed by serving dessert. "You like John Wayne movies?" Her tone indicated surprise and wariness.

"Especially the Westerns." Gabe laughed lightly and

shrugged. "I'm sure that brands me as some sort of macho throwback, but I can't help myself. I don't really care about the man's personal life or his politics. I just like the movies."

The beginning of a smile tugged at one corner of Cass's lips. "I would never have guessed that about you."

"Why not? Don't all little boys want to grow up to be cowboys?"

"And most little girls, too, these days. I would have thought with your background, though—" Cass broke off, suddenly unwilling to emphasize their differences at the cost of the fragile accord they had achieved.

"You think seven-year-old boys dream of wearing gray pin-striped suits and sitting in the corporate boardroom? Where is the romance and adventure in that?" Gabe leaned forward across the counter and fixed Cass with a serious look. "Where are the *horses?*"

Cass giggled and smacked her forehead with one hand. "Of course. How silly of me to have forgotten about that." She handed Gabe his plate. "What time does your movie start?"

Gabe glanced at his watch. "An hour or so. But I told you, it isn't important."

"You could watch it here."

Again Gabe had to admire how hard Cass was trying to be friendly to someone who had only caused her problems. It was possible she was trying to manipulate him, to disarm his suspicions and convince him of her honesty. But when he looked into her sad hazel eyes, the explanation seemed much simpler. "It must be lonely for you without Crudley around."

She flinched slightly at having been caught revealing too much of herself. She picked up her plate and walked into the living room. "I know that must sound foolish.

Neurotic." She settled onto the sofa with her legs tucked underneath her, poking absently at her food.

Gabe followed, sitting in the chair next to her. "Don't forget," he said softly, "that my standard of comparison for normal behavior around animals is Emilie Crosswhite. Believe me, you're a paradigm of sanity." When that brought a tentative smile to Cass's face, he continued. "After what you told me earlier about how long you've been together, it would be—" Gabe stopped himself just in time, before he used the accusatory word *suspicious*. "It would be remarkable if you didn't miss him," he concluded.

The gratitude in Cass's expression made Gabe feel all the guiltier that his motives were not as guileless as he was leading her to believe. Maybe, he thought hopefully, maybe for tonight he could be the nice guy she momentarily assumed he was. Maybe he could forget the past and the future and just live in the moment. If Cass was up to something dishonest, he would find out about it soon enough. If she wasn't, then she desperately needed whatever kindness and compassion he could offer.

Chapter Six

Cass's secretary buzzed her on the intercom, interrupting a confused reverie featuring Gabe Preston and Crudley. "Yes, Annie?" Cass said absently.

"Mr. Denmore would like to see you in his office as soon as possible," Annie's disembodied voice informed her.

"Okay, thanks," Cass answered, still preoccupied.

The kidnappers would be contacting Emilie Crosswhite tomorrow. Tonight Cass would have to talk to Gabe about arranging to be present when the call came in.

Tonight. Cass assumed she would be seeing Gabe again this evening. In three short days he'd become a fixture in her small apartment, and her life. She thought about last night and how he had stayed late, playing cards with her, watching an old movie on television and generally keeping her entertained...

"We don't have to watch John Wayne," he had volunteered early on.

"I love John Wayne movies. I would probably have ended up watching anyway."

"For the horses? Or for the cowboys?" Gabe had asked playfully.

"For the stories," she had informed him decisively. "I like seeing all the old-fashioned values—love and honor and loyalty—win in the end."

"No wonder you like John Wayne."

"I can even do the voice," she had told him proudly.

"Let me hear it."

"I can't do it on command," she had said, blushing at the thought of demonstrating such a ridiculous talent to someone like Gabe Preston.

"Will you do it later, during the movie?"

"I don't know." What had possessed her to tell Gabe about this?

"Come on. You have to do it now that you've teased me. I won't make you nervous by staring at you or anything. You just pick your spot and say something in your John Wayne voice."

What could she do? She had to agree. But in spite of Gabe's assurance, she was jittery as a schoolgirl waiting to perform on stage. Finally, during a lull in the dialogue of *She Wore A Yellow Ribbon,* Cass took a deep breath and said in her best imitation accent, "Did ya figger ta stop me from goin'?"

Gabe looked over at her and said "What?"

"That was it. That was my John Wayne voice."

"That was John Wayne? I thought you were doing Shirley Temple."

"Shirley Temple! I suppose you can do better?"

"I never claimed I could do the voice. I can do the walk, though."

"You do the walk? John Wayne's walk?"

"Yep."

"Let me see."

"You'll be embarrassed. You'll be asking yourself how you could claim to do a John Wayne imitation when you were in the presence of a master who humbly held his silence."

"You'd better be able to walk the walk to back up that talk."

"I can walk it."

"You'd better do it."

Sighing resignedly and casting a pitying look at Cass, Gabe stood, hitched up his jeans and swaggered across her living room and back. He stopped in front of her, one hand cocked on his hip, one shoulder dropped in a classic poster pose. "Well?" he said self-confidently.

"Now *that* was Shirley Temple."

Gabe picked up one of her couch pillows and tossed it at her. Laughing, she fended it off, picked it up and threw it right back. The fight was on. A few breathless minutes later, the couch was a shambles and both Cass and Gabe were giggling like naughty children. For a moment, the charged air seemed electrified by more than high spirits and good humor. For a moment, Cass had half expected Gabe to kiss her. Or was that only wishful thinking?

Cass dragged her thoughts back to the present. Gabe hadn't kissed her. He had been a perfect gentleman in that respect. Still, he'd seemed reluctant to leave. She'd been reluctant to see him leave. When he was around, she could almost forget about Crudley's plight for a little while.

Cass sighed. Yes, Gabe Preston was really quite charming, when he wasn't spying on her or accusing her of foul play. Recalling some of their more unpleasant confrontations brought her sharply back to the present. He was not a man she should be daydreaming about, especially with so much else to concern her. Crudley's problem was on hold until the kidnappers called back. Meanwhile, work was piling up on her desk. And what was it Annie had buzzed about just now?

For a moment Cass stopped breathing. The vice president of the company wanted to see her. What on earth for? He never dealt personally with the lower-level staff. In the two years since she'd been hired, she'd never even spoken to Mr. Denmore beyond a word or two in passing. Now she'd been summoned to his office.

Cass mentally scanned a list of her possible misdeeds. Had someone expressed dissatisfaction with her work? Had she been so distracted she'd made errors in her accounts?

It was pointless to speculate, unnerving to delay the inevitable. The receptionist outside Mr. Denmore's office motioned Cass to go right in. Knocking firmly on the heavy door, Cass straightened her shoulders and entered with feigned confidence.

Mr. Denmore sat behind a huge oak desk, barren of all but the most basic accoutrements of power. He favored Cass with a nod and brief tightening of his lips meant to pass as a smile. "Have a seat, Miss Appleton," he said, indicating one of the chairs in front of his desk. "Would you care for some coffee or tea?"

Cass sat stiff-backed in the unpadded armchair. "No, thank you."

Mr. Denmore took off his glasses and placed them on his desk, leaning backward as if to distance himself from her. "I don't have much occasion to interfere in the daily affairs of our junior employees," he said, "but in this case, I felt I had no choice."

Cass's stomach lurched and fluttered. Her heart began to pound as though she'd run ten miles. If Mr. Denmore fired her, how would she ever find another job? All her savings would be gone, spent in rescuing Crudley. She would be penniless and without any prospect for future employment. Cass broke into a cold sweat. This was the fate she had sacrificed so much to avoid.

"Emilie Crosswhite called me this morning. She indicated that you and she have a 'personal' relationship, which led her to make a somewhat unusual request. She would like you to audit the household accounts. She has discovered certain irregularities in their use. For her own reasons she prefers to keep her suspicions to herself at the present time. Hence, her request for your assistance, rather than that of her regular accounting firm or the police."

Mr. Denmore replaced his glasses and peered intently at Cass. "I assured her our discretion could be relied upon completely. I also informed her that you were available whenever she wished you to begin. There is nothing you are currently involved with that cannot be postponed."

The casual acknowledgment of the inconsequential nature of the work she did stung, even in the midst of her confusion. Mr. Denmore leaned forward, intensifying his gaze. "Let me be quite frank," he said. "This type of favor, performed for someone of Emilie Crosswhite's status, could prove very important to Laughlin and Denmore, and to your future with us."

It was not precisely a threat, but Cass knew the unspoken corollary—mess this up and you're out. "I'll do my best," she said faintly. Mr. Denmore frowned. "You can count on me," she added a little more forcefully. "I won't let you down."

Another tight-lipped smile from the vice president rewarded her final promise. "Good," he said. "For the next few days, for as long as it takes, you will be working exclusively for Mrs. Crosswhite at her estate. She's expecting you tonight for dinner at seven. She'll send her car to pick you up. Remember to be discreet. Any questions?'' Cass shook her head mutely and Mr. Denmore nodded to indicate she was dismissed.

Outside in the hallway Cass leaned against a wall for support and tried to make sense of what had just happened. This is just what I need, she thought. An opportunity to ruin my entire career. If someone *is* embezzling from Mrs. Crosswhite and he knows what he's doing, it could be almost impossible to track down. It would have to be someone she trusts, which means it's probably someone she likes, in which case she doesn't want to hear from me that the person is a thief. She'll want to get rid of the bearer of bad tidings as soon as possible, not begin a long-term relationship. Mr. Denmore won't like that at all. He'll assume the offense is my doing and fire me. At best he'll keep me on staff but bore me to death with work even more trivial than I've been doing.

I will not think about it, Cass told herself forcefully. I'm going to get my cat back, find Mrs. Crosswhite's thief and earn a glowing recommendation from her that will keep Mr. Denmore happy. I just have to take control.

With her renewed attitude firmly in place, Cass buckled down to the work at hand. She cleared up the business that, if not critical, at least needed prompt attention. Then she prioritized the rest to attend to when she returned from Crosswhite Manor.

As she stood up to leave, she scanned her sterile surroundings, void of any sign of personality or even humanity. The right job, the right clothes, the right address—they had seemed to be prerequisites to achieving the safe stable life she yearned for. In her quest for that life, she'd forsaken her talent and buried her individuality. The one thing she would never sacrifice was Crudley.

Now was no time for futile soul-searching. She had to stop by the bank on the way home and pick up the ransom money to be prepared when the kidnappers called tomorrow.

Gabe Preston's car was noticeably absent from the street in front of her house when she pulled into her driveway at half-past five. Not trusting the visual evidence, she listened outside her door for sounds of another unauthorized intrusion. She heard nothing, and when she unlocked the door everything looked exactly as she'd left it. Perhaps knowing that in a little while Mrs. Crosswhite's chauffeur would be picking her up had convinced Gabe not to waste his time staking out her apartment for only an hour or so. The unexpected, though small, show of faith in her pleased Cass. She smiled as she shed her clothes and headed for the shower.

The cooling spray pulsed against her skin. She tried to concentrate on the sensation rather than the task she'd been summoned to perform for Emilie Crosswhite. Conjecture was useless. Cass barely knew by sight any of the household staff other than Gabe. She couldn't even guess how many employees would be in a position to embezzle from their employer, let alone which ones.

Except, of course, for Gabe Preston. Emilie obviously trusted him and cared for him. But on what was the wealthy matron's confidence founded? A long-standing relationship between the generations of two families? Every family had its black sheep. Was Gabe the scoundrel in the Preston clan?

Cass knew almost nothing about the man, really. Gabe had shown an intense curiosity about her life while remaining extraordinarily reticent about his own. The details of his personal history were completely unknown. Where had he grown up? Did he have any brothers or sisters?

What had he done before he went to work for his godmother?

Cass turned off the water and scowled, realizing how successfully Gabe had hidden his past from her. Even when she'd confronted him with direct questions, he'd merely shrugged or offered some evasive or noncommittal reply and turned the inquiry back on her.

Yet in spite of his secretiveness about his past, Cass felt she knew Gabe Preston. Even if his family had lost all its money, Gabe would not have resorted to embezzling from Emilie Crosswhite. If, as Mr. Denmore had said, Mrs. Crosswhite had confided her suspicions to no one else, including her chief of security, it could not be due to any lack of faith in Gabe.

Gabe could not disguise his true character merely by failing to disclose the events that had shaped the man he'd become. Cass understood why Emilie Crosswhite trusted Gabe. She only wished her own feelings were so uncomplicated and easy to understand.

After toweling off, Cass chose a simple but elegant gray silk shirt and pants from her closet. The fabric shimmered like liquid silver flowing over the curves of her body and always made her feel sensual and vibrantly alive. She brushed her dark hair vigorously, trying to smooth the capricious curls into the sleek style they'd been cut to hold. It was useless. With a resigned toss of her head, Cass shook the last remnants of sophisticated fashion from her hair and watched the dark waves fall in a more natural position, framing her face.

The sound of the door chimes startled her. Cass glanced at the clock. It was barely past six. Perhaps Mrs. Crosswhite expected her for cocktails, too. She should probably have called her hostess back and confirmed all the details of her engagement tonight, but she still didn't know the phone number at Crosswhite Manor. So far it hadn't mattered. She'd been in constant touch with Emilie's employee, if she'd needed a message relayed. Grabbing a delicate silver chain for her neck and matching bracelet, Cass slipped them into her purse and went to answer the door.

She'd been prepared to greet the uniformed stranger entrusted with chauffeuring her to the estate. Instead, she found Gabe Preston slouched casually against the porch railing. His inspection of her appearance took just fractionally longer than professional interest dictated. Cass stared back at him with mixed consternation and pleasure.

"You look terrific," Gabe said.

Warmth flooded through Cass's entire body. "Thank you," she said shyly.

Gabe smiled at her apparent self-consciousness. "Surely the compliment can't be that unusual?"

"I...I was expecting someone else."

It was Gabe's turn to look perplexed. "Didn't Emilie reach you at your office?"

"Yes, but—"

"Didn't she invite you for dinner tonight?"

"It was passed on to me as more of a command, actually. But—"

"But you already had other plans," Gabe finished for her. He cast another, more thoughtful look at Cass's outfit. "I should have realized you're dressed for more arousing company than a society matron. Or her chief of security." His voice held an edge that accented the sudden flash of cold fire in his eyes.

"If you think I'm dressed inappropriately, I can change," Cass said defensively. The tilt of her chin dared him to repeat the criticism. "All I was trying to say, before you began leaping to conclusions, was that I expected

Mrs. Crosswhite to send her chauffeur to pick me up. Not you."

"Oh." Gabe eased back against the porch railing, resuming his casual manner. He grinned sheepishly. "In that case, you're dressed perfectly. Hand me your suitcase and we'll get going."

"What suitcase?"

"Duffel bag, brown paper sack—whatever you've packed the rest of your clothes in."

Cass sighed and pressed her fingertips to her temples. "I'm beginning to feel like Alice in Wonderland. Why do I need more clothes? Have you planned some bizarre after-dinner entertainment? If it's polo, I'm afraid it's too late for me to rent a horse for the evening."

"Emilie should never be allowed to make her own arrangements with normal people who don't know her." Gabe's grin was rueful, but tinged with affection for the object of his disclaimer. "I take it that Emilie somehow neglected to mention that she's planned to put you up at the house for the next few days, until this whole business with Crudley is settled?"

Cass brushed a wayward curl from her forehead. "No, she didn't mention anything about me staying at Crosswhite Manor. Or rather," Cass corrected, "if she mentioned it, I wasn't told. It's my fault, really. All my information came secondhand, through my boss. Mrs. Crosswhite called to ask—"

Cass's internal warning system belatedly alerted her to the danger of explaining any further. Even if Gabe weren't a suspect himself, even if Emilie Crosswhite had taken him into her confidence on this issue, it was not something he and Cass should be discussing.

"—to ask me to come to the estate," Cass finished lamely. "I guess I was preoccupied and didn't listen very closely. I'll just put a few things in a suitcase. It won't take me a minute."

As she hurriedly collected a few changes of clothes and laid them on the bed, Cass wondered how she was going to find a minute to talk with Emilie Crosswhite in private, away from the ever-present ever-vigilant Gabe Preston. He seemed to come and go as he pleased, and the past few days he'd made sticking with Cass his personal mission.

Why should anything be easy? she thought ruefully, surveying the assortment of garments she'd assembled. And what do I pack for a stay of two or three days at the estate of one of Newport's wealthiest widows? Jeans and T-shirts? Business suits? I'm fresh out of evening gowns since I outgrew my prom dress.

So far she'd gathered only casual clothes. She removed the ransom money from her briefcase and put it in her overnight bag, then folded her clothes on top. After adding a few toiletries, she closed the lid firmly on this minor problem. If she needed anything else, surely the chauffeur or Gabe would bring her back to fetch it.

"All set," she announced to Gabe, handing him the suitcase.

He eyed the bag speculatively. "Did you really squeeze a polo pony in there?" he asked.

"The pony was a cinch. It was the mallet that gave me trouble," she shot back, breezing by him to the door. "Coming?"

"Yes, ma'am!"

The evening air was still uncomfortably warm, but Gabe apparently had traded the beige sedan for a sporty silver Jaguar, which was bound to have air-conditioning. "Yours?" Cass asked blandly, barely lifting one eyebrow.

"Mine," Gabe agreed. "At least until midnight. Then

it turns back into a pumpkin. If you decide to leave after that, you'll have to ride the polo pony."

"And what do *you* turn into at midnight?"

Gabe feigned surprise as he opened the car door for Cass. "Me? I thought we'd already established that. I'm a toad."

Cass paused before getting in the Jaguar. "You're mixing up your fairy tales. The driver of the pumpkin coach isn't a toad. He's a rat."

"Now you're confused. The driver isn't a rat, he's a pleasant harmless little mouse. But I'm sure that I'm right about me being a toad. I'm positive that if you'd kiss me, I'd turn into Prince Charming."

Cass laughed despite herself. "Nice try. But the story is called 'The Frog Prince,' not 'The Toad Prince.' All I can get from kissing a toad is warts."

Gabe looked thoughtful. "I think you're wrong." He leaned close to Cass and smiled in a way that sent shivers through her. His breath seared her cheek. "Maybe," he said softly, "we should do an experiment and see exactly what does happen. We don't even have to wait until midnight." His dark lashes shadowed his cheeks as his gaze dropped deliberately to her lips.

Conflicting emotions temporarily immobilized Cass. Fighting the all but irresistible desire to follow Gabe's suggestion, she ducked into the car. Her face still burned from Gabe's mere proximity. In fact, her whole body felt inflamed. "Can we get going please?" she asked irritably. She couldn't look at Gabe, certain he wore the wide grin that had become his perpetual expression around her.

The ride to Crosswhite Manor passed in tense silence for Cass as she mentally lectured herself about the dangers of falling in love with a man like Gabe Preston. She barely knew him. She wasn't even sure she liked him. She was kidding herself if she thought he was anything but an aristocratic playboy amusing himself by flirting with the lower classes.

The object of her silent berating remained unmoved by her inner turmoil. He whistled softly in accompaniment to the light classical music on the radio while expertly maneuvering the sports car through the narrow back streets of Newport. At Crosswhite Manor he took the service driveway, stopping outside the gate where he and Cass had first met. Turning to her, he asked "Shall I open it or would you prefer to climb?"

Still flustered by his earlier flirting and the feelings it had provoked, Cass refused to reply. Gabe grinned at her a moment longer, then shrugged and pressed a remote-control unit to activate the entry.

The garage where Gabe parked the Jaguar held five other vehicles, all shined and presumably ready to go. Cass wondered if Emilie Crosswhite even knew how to drive, or if that was one of the harsh realities the late Hartley Crosswhite had protected her from.

On the wide expanse of asphalt adjoining the garage, half a dozen children played boisterous basketball. Their shouts in a variety of unfamiliar languages supported Gabe's explanation of Emilie's multicultural hiring practices. Nearby a man on a huge lawn tractor worked his way up and down the back acreage. Gabe lightly placed his hand at the small of Cass's back, guiding her down a tree-lined walk to the main house.

They entered through the kitchen. Eva, the housekeeper, stood center stage, calmly but firmly issuing instructions to a pair of youthful waiters. Heavenly aromas emanated from stove and oven, which were tended by two cooks in immaculate white. Gabe hustled Cass out of everyone's way and into the dining room, then on to a huge room where a dozen or so people milled around in small groups, talking and sipping cocktails or wine.

Perhaps because of the circumstances underlying the invitation, Cass had assumed dinner would be a small private affair involving only herself and Emilie Crosswhite, and possibly Gabe Preston. She was relieved that her silky gray outfit's casual elegance seemed to fit in with everyone else's attire. Except Gabe's, she noted. In crisp white shirt and tan pants he was a bit underdressed. On the other hand, she grudgingly admitted, he looked terrific. Bronzed skin, sun-streaked hair and that killer smile were all he would ever need to be the most attractive man wherever he went.

Gabe caught her staring at him as he turned away from the bar carrying two wineglasses. The killer smile widened as he sauntered in her direction. "I think you'll find this a sultry little vintage," he said, handing her one of the glasses. "Ripe, spicy, with just a hint of underlying sweetness. I think it will age well, although it's perfect right now." His eyes sparkled with mischief, and something more. Cass found her mouth had gone dry, but when she raised her glass to drink, Gabe's eyes lingered on her lips.

She pivoted hastily, pretending a sudden interest in a painting on a nearby wall. As she gulped too much wine too quickly, she stared straight ahead, concentrating on the artwork in front of her to steady her racing pulse. Gradually the colors and forms of the watercolor began to intrude on her chaotic thoughts, soothing her. She actually looked at the painting for the first time.

"Like it?" Gabe asked over her shoulder. Cass could feel the heat of his body behind her, but the sensation no longer seemed threatening.

"It's exquisite," she said dreamily, allowing herself to

lean back slightly. Her shoulder brushed Gabe's chest, her hip rested lightly against his thigh. "You could be having the worst day of your life, but if you stood in front of this picture, you could forget about everything bad."

They stood in companionable silence for a few minutes. "It reminds me of your paintings," Gabe said finally. "Not so much the style as the feeling."

Cass twisted her head to look at him. "Thank you. That's very flattering, whether or not you meant it to be. This artist was a genius."

"I can believe that. I also believe the only significant difference between his work and yours is that he's reaching out to people, while you're trying to shut them out."

Cass stiffened and stepped away, her defenses rising. "I didn't realize you're such an expert on art," she said icily.

"I'm not talking about art. I'm talking about you. That's a subject I *am* becoming quite an expert on. I talked to Seth Gratton today." Cass whirled to face him, her hand clenched around the wineglass stem. "He remembers you very well," Gabe continued, "because not many people refuse the opportunity to display their works in his gallery. He even remembers the exact words you used when you turned him down. 'I can't make a living selling my dreams.' He was never quite sure how to interpret that."

"How dare you?" Cass whispered with barely controlled rage, practically strangling her wineglass. "How dare you pry into my personal life, interrogating every casual acquaintance whose path ever crossed mine?"

"You brought this on yourself," Gabe reminded her wearily. "You know I've been investigating you."

"I thought you were checking my professional credentials, verifying my employment, doing the kinds of things a bank or a credit-card company does. You have no right to harass the people I know."

"I have every right to protect Emilie. You're here in her house, essentially a complete stranger she's chosen to treat like a friend. Don't lecture me about my rights or responsibilities."

"What about your manners? What about common decency? What about my right to privacy? You need to be lectured on those topics. You—"

"Gabriel, darling!" a warm cheery voice interrupted. "You're not fighting with my guest, are you?"

Chapter Seven

Cass took a deep breath, glared at Gabe one final second, then forced a smile as she greeted her hostess. "Mrs. Crosswhite. Thank you for inviting me. I was just admiring this wonderful painting."

"I see. Then you and Gabriel were having an artistic difference of opinion. I always thought you liked this painting, too, dear," she said innocently to Gabe.

"I do," he said smoothly. "But you know how emotional some people get about art."

Cass fumed silently, wondering how much Emilie knew about Gabe's investigative methods. Had Mrs. Crosswhite consented to this wholesale trespass on her life? It was difficult to believe this sweet little woman had. It was equally difficult to believe Gabe would do anything his patroness expressly forbid.

"You look lovely, dear." Mrs. Crosswhite took Cass's free hand and gently unlocked the fingers of the fist Cass had unconsciously formed. "I was afraid you might not get my message in time to make it tonight. When I called,

I asked for Conrad Laughlin. He and I have met once or twice. Apparently Conrad is out of town at the moment, so they gave me to that Mr. Denmore. He didn't seem to know who you were at first, dear. I certainly hope he doesn't have many children. He can't seem to keep track of even small quantities of people very well."

Cass's anger faded as she grinned in appreciation of Emilie's perfectly modulated barb. It would be a mistake for anyone to dismiss this woman's guileless manner as simple naiveté.

Mrs. Crosswhite continued assessing Cass's appearance. Given how Cass looked the last time Emilie saw her, straight from a hot drive and a brisk climb over a high iron fence, Cass assumed the comparison was favorable.

"Yes, you do look lovely, dear," Emilie said. "That color complements your beautiful complexion. In fact… Wait right here, dear. Well, of course you'll wait. You haven't even had dinner yet. Gabriel, entertain Miss Appleton for a few minutes, will you please? Show her the rest of the artwork. I'm sure she'll enjoy that. Only keep away from any controversial pieces, won't you? You'll both upset your digestion, and really, it's all a matter of personal taste. Like falling in love," she added, smiling benignly first at Cass, than at Gabe. She floated away in a swirl of chiffon.

Cass blushed furiously. Had Mrs. Crosswhite seen her almost leaning against Gabe? Did she think she'd interrupted a lovers' quarrel? Or was Cass's weakness painfully obvious to everyone? She'd always prided herself on being able to control her emotions. Lately, however, she didn't seem able to repress or restrain any of her feelings. Her failure wasn't only embarrassing, it was dangerous.

For Crudley's sake, she had to master her anger at the very least.

Cass flinched as Gabe touched her elbow. She quickly took a few steps away, unable to meet his eyes. Neither of them spoke as they dutifully worked their way around the perimeter of the room studying Emilie's art collection. When they stopped in front of a still life in blue tones, Cass moved closer to read the artist's signature.

"Like it?" Gabe asked conversationally.

"It's good," Cass admitted with some surprise. "It must be one of his early pieces."

"How can you tell?"

"He doesn't paint like that anymore." Both envy and regret shaded her words. She took another long sip of wine.

"Indeed, he doesn't," Emilie chimed in as she rejoined Cass and Gabe. "I bought this eleven years ago, before he became popular."

"And when he still had a soul to go with all that technique," Cass added.

"Ouch!" Gabe said, stepping forward to look more closely at the painting. "Wait a minute. Even I have heard of this guy. One of his paintings sold at a local charity auction the other night for twenty thousand dollars."

"Twenty-three thousand," Emilie corrected. "The painting was *Octet*."

Cass sighed and shook her head. "I've seen the painting. Whoever bought it was robbed. At least it was for a good cause."

"The robbery victim is here tonight," Gabe murmured, "standing just over there." He inclined his head toward a group of men in subdued conversation about ten feet away. "Perhaps you'd like to explain to him the error of his ways?"

Cass threw a guilty look over her shoulder. "Perhaps I'd like to lower my voice," she said, "and keep my opinions to myself." And drink less wine, she added silently, setting her empty glass down on a nearby table to avoid temptation.

"Nonsense, dear." Emilie patted her hand reassuringly. "William Dalbrie doesn't know anything about art, including what he likes!" She laughed gaily at her own joke.

It was impossible not to laugh with her. Emilie Crosswhite was definitely the perfect hostess, Cass thought gratefully. She put you at ease and forgave you all your social blunders. "You've very kind," Cass said softly, hardly aware she'd spoken aloud until Emilie's smile softened and she patted Cass's hand again.

"I almost forgot!" Emilie said suddenly. She reached into a pocket hidden in the billows of chiffon surrounding the tiny figure. She pulled out a small velvet box and handed it to Cass. "I thought of this the moment I saw you shimmering next to Gabriel."

Cass opened the box. Inside was an antique silver locket with delicate floral etching.

"It was my grandmother's," Emilie continued. "She had your same coloring and dark hair. Put it on, dear. Gabriel, help her with the clasp."

Gabe set his wineglass next to Cass's and removed the locket from the box. Then he stood behind her and gently lifted her hair off her neck. His fingertips brushed sensitive skin and Cass shivered. She pushed his hands away and reached up to secure her hair herself, hoping to minimize the physical contact with Gabe. But as he ostensibly fumbled with the clasp to the locket, his hands caressed her nape and his fingers twined through escaped tendrils of her hair. Head bowed, Cass closed her eyes and willed the ordeal to end, half hoping it never would.

Completing the task at last, Gabe rested his hands lightly on her shoulders. The cool metal of the locket warmed quickly against Cass's overheated skin. She raised her head and opened her eyes to Emilie's blissfully approving expression.

"The perfect finishing touch. Don't you think so, Gabriel?"

"Perfect touch," Gabe agreed.

Cass tried to slip out of his persistent grasp. In response he subtly tightened his hold. Cass was sure if she struggled or slipped him a quick elbow in the ribs, she could escape. But she'd already created one minor scene and made an indiscreet remark about another guest's taste in art. She was over her own limit for bad behavior during one dinner party.

"Emilie, I don't believe I've met this lovely lady," a voice said on Cass's left.

"I haven't had the opportunity to introduce her around yet, William. Cass Appleton, this is William Dalbrie. William, Miss Appleton."

The handshake he offered was firm and brief. The man himself was tall and slender, wearing a beautifully tailored suit that undoubtedly cost more than Cass earned in a month. A touch of gray in his smooth dark hair only added to his air of distinction. "I hear you're something of an expert on art," he said to Cass.

Her stomach lurched. He must have overheard her comment about his recently acquired painting.

"I told William I'd invited a friend of mine who's an artist," Emilie hurriedly assured Cass. "He's been looking forward to meeting you. Gabriel, dear, would you help me with something in the other room?"

The determined look in Emilie's eyes precluded any argument Gabe might have made. Reluctantly he released Cass and took Emilie's arm. As they crossed the room, Gabe looked down at his tiny godmother. "Do you think it's a good idea to leave Cass alone back there?"

"Why not? She's a lovely intelligent cultured young woman. Don't worry so much about her. She'll be fine."

"I was thinking about your other guests. Cass has some pretty negative preconceptions about wealthy blue-blooded types like your friends."

"Including you, dear?"

"She dislikes me for a number of reasons. That's only one of them."

"I'm sure you're mistaken about Cass's feelings. She's been confused and upset the past few days because of poor Crudley's kidnapping. She may have said and done things she regrets. She may even have lashed out at the people trying to help her. But she is, at heart, a lady. She would never dream of insulting any of my guests. Now help me find Eva."

A short while later when dinner was called, Gabe discovered someone had rearranged the table setting. He was in his accustomed place next to Mrs. Crosswhite, who sat at the head of the table. But instead of Cass being opposite him, on Emilie's other side, her place card was now at the far end of the table. She would be surrounded by strangers throughout the entire meal.

Gabe felt a small pang of anxiety on her behalf. Despite what he'd said to Emilie, he didn't like thinking of the reclusive Cass thrown into an unfamiliar social whirl among people she probably assumed considered her inferior.

Gabe need not have worried. Cass came into the room on the arm of Emilie's cousin Edgar, the retired former owner of an international shipping line who still sat on the executive boards of at least half a dozen companies. The two of them chatted easily together while they found their seats. As the dinner progressed, the soft lilting sound of Cass's laughter frequently floated above the conversation at her end of the table.

"She's the belle of the ball, isn't she?" Emilie said to Gabe as dessert was served.

"She deserves to be. I doubt she's had many other opportunities."

"I'm sorry you're stuck with boring old me." Emilie patted Gabe's hand affectionately.

Gabe smiled fondly at her. "You're never boring, Emilie. Anyway, I'm sure Cass is having a better time without me lurking around like an unwanted chaperon. I always seem to make her angry."

"Your lack of faith in her makes her understandably angry. And since she obviously finds you attractive, your not trusting her makes it even worse."

"There's nothing I can do about it."

"About what? Her attraction to you? Your doubts about her? Or your attraction to her?"

Gabe sighed heavily. "Don't go borrowing trouble, Emilie. Until this ransom problem is resolved, I can't afford to worry about anyone but you."

"Life doesn't succumb to such easy compartmentalizations, Gabriel. One part won't conveniently stand still while you deal with another part. Cass won't wait forever for you to decide she's trustworthy. And she may not forgive you for refusing to commit yourself until all the proof is in."

"That's a chance I'll have to take."

"Not on my account," Emilie said emphatically. "I tell you now I have absolute and complete faith in that girl.

She is incapable of deceiving anyone, except possibly herself, and I have high hopes of remedying that."

Gabe stared down the length of the table at Cass. Her face was angled slightly in his direction as she listened intently to one of her dinner companions. Candlelight softened the contours of her cheeks and a shy smile tilted the corners of her mouth.

"Failing to trust the right person can be just as great a mistake as trusting the wrong one, Gabriel."

"I know, Emilie," he said, watching Cass unconsciously slide her fingertips along the silver chain at her throat. "I just wish I knew which mistake I'm making this time."

The evening ended too soon for Cass. As Emilie closed the door behind the last departing guest, she turned and beamed at Cass. "I expect you could have carried on until dawn, my dear."

"Everyone was so nice to me," Cass said, the wonder evident in her voice. "You were very kind to invite me. I've never been to a lovelier party."

"What a sweet thing to say! Now that we're all becoming such good friends, you must come over for dinner more often."

Gabe cleared his throat from somewhere behind Cass. She ignored him, sure from the impish look on Emilie's face that she would meet disapproval on Gabe's. "I'd like that," she said sincerely.

"Good. Now I really must say good-night. I have some kind of meeting in the morning, and I need my full eight hours sleep or I make no sense at all. Gabriel, will you show Cass to her room?"

"I'm going to check with Paul and make sure the grounds are secured for the night. Eva can show her."

As if by magic, Eva materialized at Cass's side. "Come with me, please, Miss Appleton."

"Thank you again, Mrs. Crosswhite," Cass said.

"I'll see you in the morning, dear."

Eva led Cass down a series of corridors and up a flight of stairs to a spacious beautifully furnished bedroom. Cass's tiny suitcase stood near an antique dressing table on which her toiletries had been arranged.

"If you need anything, please ring," Eva instructed her, indicating an old-fashioned bellpull by the door. "Or you can use the house phone." Cass nodded, slightly overwhelmed by the thought of summoning a servant. She didn't even like to use room service when she stayed at a hotel.

After Eva left, Cass kicked off her shoes and collapsed on the bed, replaying the evening in her mind. The other guests were not at all what she'd expected. She couldn't remember ever being so comfortable in a group of strangers. She'd assumed she would have nothing in common with any of Emilie's friends and consequently nothing to talk about. Yet the time had flown by. Everyone had been warm and gracious, interested in Cass's ideas and opinions, and unconcerned that she clearly was not one of their social set.

Only Gabe Preston seemed out of sync with the group. He brooded increasingly through dinner, apparently determined to maintain his emotional distance from the festivities. Cass suspected she was the reason for his watchfulness. She had sensed his scrutiny all night. Whenever she glanced his way and made eye contact, his expression revealed nothing of what he was thinking.

Cass sat up and swept her hair off her forehead as if the gesture would clear her mind. Her relationship with Gabe Preston was becoming more problematic by the hour. Three days ago she'd been certain she knew all about him. He was one of the idle rich, fighting off boredom by amusing himself "working" for his godmother as head of security on her estate. Since then, Cass had been compelled to reconsider her conclusions.

The one thing she had no doubt about was Gabe's affection for Emilie. His feelings for herself were another matter. In the time she'd known him, he'd been baiting her and flirting with her, suspecting and admiring her in equal measure, probably to deliberately keep her off balance. She thought she felt a strong attraction between them hovering around the edges of every encounter, but was inclined to think she could be mistaking the intensity of their situation for an intensity of emotion that didn't exist.

Cass stood up and paced restlessly in front of the bed. She wasn't exactly an expert when it came to men. Her mother's example had made her leery of relationships in general. Throughout school she had avoided any serious entanglements, keeping her friendships with men strictly that. After she graduated, she'd concentrated on paying off her loans and gaining her professional credentials. She'd had little time to pursue an active social life.

She hadn't regretted her choices at the time. She didn't regret them now. But she did feel ill equipped to deal with the quicksand of male-female interactions. She thought again of her mother's multiple disastrous romances, only some of which had culminated in unfortunate marriages. Maybe experience wasn't that good a teacher, anyway. On the other hand, if heredity was destiny, she was doomed.

Vain speculations had dissipated the after-party glow for Cass. She couldn't sleep with so many unanswered questions whirling in her thoughts. Nothing could be done about her personal problems at the moment. But perhaps she could make a start on her professional one. She checked the grandfather clock guarding her room. It hadn't been long since they had said good-night downstairs. Maybe Mrs. Crosswhite was still awake, and alone at last. If she could have just a moment to speak to her about the possible embezzlement, she might be able to focus on that to the exclusion of all the other insoluble issues battering her heart and mind.

It was worth a try. For one thing she was unlikely to find a better opportunity to speak confidentially to her new client without arousing notice from potential suspects. If she accidentally encountered anyone, she could explain that she was going for a moonlight stroll in the gardens.

Cass picked up her shoes and carried them with her as she cautiously opened the guest bedroom door and peered into the hallway. Closing it softly behind her, she tried to draw a mental map of what she knew about the layout of the estate. Mrs. Crosswhite's private quarters were, she'd been told, in the east wing, overlooking the rear of the estate and near the morning room where Cass had first entered the house.

Cass started down the hallway in what she thought was the right direction. She turned left at the first corridor—and almost tripped over Gabe Preston's legs. He was leaning against the wall, arms folded across his chest, eyeing her with cool skepticism. "Going somewhere?"

"F-for a walk," Cass stammered. "In the garden."

"Good thing you brought your shoes."

Cass didn't need to wonder if she looked as guilty as she felt. Heat burned in her cheeks and her heart pounded furiously. Of all the bad luck! Why did she have to run into the one person she most hoped to avoid—and the one who would naturally assume the worst about her nocturnal prowl?

But was it luck? What had Gabe been doing in the corridor before she ran into him? The answer seemed painfully obvious to her, especially in her already skittish state. "Don't you have anything better to do than spy on me? I wasn't going to filch the family silverware or jewelry," she said haughtily.

"You didn't bring enough luggage for that. Besides, the perimeter of the property is patroled with dogs at night. Even you would have a tough time making it over the fence after dark."

Cass ignored the flippant reference. "Then why are you lurking around in the hallway?" she demanded.

"Maybe I'm not. Maybe I was on my way to ask you if you wanted to go for a walk in the gardens when I heard you coming."

Gabe took advantage of her flustered silence to claim her hand and begin leading her down the corridor. He took what looked like a servants' staircase, guiding Cass through unfamiliar territory in a part of the house she hadn't seen before. Despite their confusing route, Cass was certain they were going in the wrong direction. She was formulating a protest when they approached a set of curtained French doors opening onto a huge terrace overlooking acres of well-manicured gardens.

"Put on your shoes," Gabe instructed.

Cass had never been on this side of the estate. Gabe led her away from the lights of the house to a secluded section of the grounds boxed in by tall hedges. They sat down on a marble bench amid beds of pale flowers in a dozen varieties. Moonlight cast an ethereal glow over everything. Cass felt as though she'd been transported to another world. "This is incredible," she murmured.

"The Bridal Garden," Gabe explained. "All the flowers are white. Most of them are associated by either name or tradition with weddings. Hartley Crosswhite planted and maintained this himself while he was still alive. Now Emilie looks after it, with a little help from her friends."

It seemed impossible to hold on to negative emotions in this setting. A feeling of calm stole over Cass as she contemplated the garden. The person who'd planned and tended the garden had known his time and effort would be rewarded. He'd known that, year after year, he or his family would be at Crosswhite Manor, where they'd always been, to enjoy its beauty. Seasons would come and seasons would go, but the Crosswhites would have this house and these grounds to anchor them in a changing world.

"It's so peaceful here," Cass said, thinking aloud. "It would be wonderful to live someplace like this."

"It is beautiful," Gabe conceded, "but don't let that blind you to the reality. It's also a prison."

The harsh word broke through Cass's enchantment. "A prison!"

Gabe made a sweeping gesture. "Look at this place. Those high iron fences aren't merely ornamental and they don't only keep trespassers out. They keep Emilie in."

"Oh, for pity's sake. She can go out anytime she wants to."

"But she can't go anywhere and do anything she wants. That's a fantasy people who aren't rich have about people who are. It isn't safe for Emilie to wander around in public. Too many people envy what she has and would try to grab a piece of it for themselves any way they could."

"Like me?" Cass said contentiously.

"You're not the first person who's climbed that fence," Gabe countered. "You're only the first one I invited."

"And you've been regretting it ever since. Believe me, if it wasn't for Crudley's welfare, I'd be regretting it, too."

"It hasn't worked out so badly for you. You seemed to be enjoying yourself at the party tonight."

"It was the most wonderful evening of my life," Cass affirmed. A rush of pleasant memories threatened to dispel her irritation with Gabe.

"Emilie knows a lot of influential people."

"They were all so nice to me," Cass said in lingering amazement at the kindness and acceptance of Emilie's friends.

"I'm sure they will prove to be useful business contacts."

Cass frowned at Gabe's vaguely antagonistic tone. "Two of them gave me their business cards in case I ever need their professional help. One of them offered to show my work in a local gallery. But I doubt—" She broke off, realizing belatedly what Gabe was implying.

"I guess you have it all figured out," she said softly. "I can't fool you. I broke into the veterinary clinic during a fake trip out of town so I could make it look as though my imaginary cat had been kidnapped, so I could meet Mrs. Emilie Crosswhite, so she would invite me to dinner where I would meet lots of rich important people who would help me advance in my career. Or was I hoping to meet a wealthy eligible male to seduce into marriage? I can't seem to remember."

Gabe sighed heavily. "What are you babbling about?"

"I'm admitting defeat. It was a nearly flawless plan, but I failed to take into account your keen analytical skills. So run! Warn all Mrs. Crosswhite's friends. A fortune hunter is on the prowl in their midst!"

Gabe glared at her a full ten seconds. "I don't know

why I brought you here," he said, losing patience with her at last. "I don't know what I could have been thinking. I don't know what I hoped for." He stood abruptly and grabbed for her hand. "Come on," he said, jerking her from the marble bench.

Gabe had miscalculated the effects of frustration and adrenaline. The tug he intended to bring Cass to her feet propelled her, instead, right into his arms. Too shocked to move, she leaned against his chest, looking up at him in wide-eyed astonishment. They stared at each other without moving.

Gabe drew a ragged breath. "I think I just remembered why I brought you here," he said.

Knowing what was coming, Cass felt the seconds pass with agonizing slowness. Gabe's hands slipped around her waist, his head bent toward her uplifted face. The desire in his eyes was almost frighteningly intense. Cass closed her eyes, like a child convinced that nothing she cannot see can touch her.

This time the tried-and-true defense failed. Gabe's lips were soft, his kiss impossibly gentle at first. He seemed to be deliberately holding back. He was waiting, Cass realized—waiting for her to decide if this was what she really wanted. His hands slid lightly around her back, and Cass pressed closer to him. She felt his body tense with yearning and knew what his control was costing him. She'd never been in more danger and she'd never felt safer. All her reservations crumbled when she realized Gabe's self-imposed restraints would protect her.

Light-headed with the new sensations flooding through her and emboldened by the power Gabe had given her, Cass twined her fingers through his hair and drew his head down, deepening the kiss. She didn't know how long it went on. She knew she wished it would never end. Gabe kissed her with complete concentration, as though it were all he wanted in the world, at least for this one moment out of time.

So completely had Cass surrendered her passion she was shocked when Gabe gently disengaged from their embrace. He held her at arm's length, obviously mastering his own longing with considerable effort. "This is not a good idea," he said finally. His voice was thick with regret and unsatisfied need.

Cass was unconcerned with anything except recovering the state of sensual intoxication she'd unwillingly relinquished. "It's the best idea we've had so far," she countered.

Gabe grinned wryly. "Yeah, it probably is. But the timing is lousy. You're confused, you're worried and you're lonely. Despite what you think of me, I don't take advantage of women who are emotionally raw and vulnerable."

"I can take care of myself," Cass automatically objected, stung by his perception of her. The brief flash of anger served to bring her to her senses. "But you're right. This isn't a good idea, regardless of the timing."

Gabe's grin tightened into a thin-lipped scowl. "Let's go in," he said. He led Cass back through the gardens, walking slightly ahead of her and carefully avoiding touching her. At the terrace he rang the servants' bell. "Someone will be here shortly to show you to your room. Good night." He turned and walked off into the shadows.

A few moments later one of the household staff did appear. A middle-aged woman who spoke slow and precise English courteously guided Cass back to her quarters.

Sleep did not come easily. Cass hadn't found what she'd gone searching for and had found something unexpected and unwanted, instead. The last thing in the world she needed was to fall in love with a man like Gabe Preston.

A man like Gabe Preston. What did that even mean? She didn't know anything about his past—who his family and friends were, where he'd grown up, what games he'd played as a child. She didn't know anything about his future. If he had dreams and ambitions, they were a mystery to her. She had to admit she didn't know much about his present, either. How had he wound up living at Crosswhite Manor and become friend and protector of Emilie Crosswhite?

Cass knew nothing about Gabe, except that for a little while in a moonlit garden, surrounded by the fragrance of late-summer flowers, the details of their separate lives hadn't mattered at all. Stripped of the complications that circumstances had imposed on their relationship, there was some fundamental magnetism between them that promised a deeper more lasting affinity than their difficult beginning together implied. Cass had the perilous feeling that if the occasion arose, she might sacrifice almost anything to be with Gabe.

Surely this wasn't the kind of feeling you could have for more than one person in a lifetime. Surely this wasn't how her mother had felt, time and time again, with each of the men who'd drifted into her life. Or was it?

Cass pressed the heels of her hands against her eyes. Much as she hated to admit it, Gabe was right about one thing. She was emotionally raw. She shouldn't be making irrevocable decisions at this point in her life. For the time being she needed to keep on his good side. But she also needed to avoid being alone with him. After Crudley was home safe, she could worry about the rest of her life.

Chapter Eight

Cass spent a restless night. Memories of kissing Gabe Preston in the garden kept her tossing and turning, her torment augmented by the possibility that the man she found so attractive was not simply a charming playboy, but possibly a seductive villain. And always, underlying all her other emotions, was the uncertainty about Crudley's fate.

A little after seven Cass gave up all pretense of sleep and dressed. The thought of ringing or phoning to ask when and where she was expected for breakfast was too bizarre. Besides, she was afraid that if she forewarned anyone she was awake and hungry, a five-course meal would arrive on her doorstep within minutes.

Instead, she wandered downstairs toward the kitchen. There she found the kitchen staff already in high gear. The air was fragrant with the smells of fresh-baked cinnamon rolls, broiled bacon and a mixture of uncountable mouthwatering scents. The activity was constant, the chatter in several languages continuous and good-natured as laughter bubbled up frequently from all concerned. The scene reminded Cass of a movie depiction of a huge family get-together on some special occasion. People came and went, jostling each other, filling their plates and returning them empty.

Eva noticed Cass poised uncertainly in the doorway. "Come on in," she said, beckoning. "Take a plate, point to whatever you want, and then I'll show you to the breakfast room, where you can eat in peace." She issued the directions automatically, no doubt aware that many visitors found the house protocol a bit strange.

Cass gamely ventured closer to the stoves to see what was at hand, dodging some of the children she'd seen playing basketball yesterday. "I definitely need one of those cinnamon rolls," she said, trying to locate the source of the aroma. A moment later a teenage girl in a white apron handed Cass a plate on which sat a warm frosted bun.

Thereafter, Cass had to battle to keep food off her dish. The two women who appeared to share head-chef duties took turns urging her to have "just a little" of everything. She escaped with her cinnamon roll, some fresh fruit, a portion of an open-faced omelette and samples of two exotic concoctions involving tomatoes and potatoes respectively.

"If I worked here, I'd weigh four hundred pounds," Cass said as Eva led her into a sunny room with a small dining table and chairs.

"Mrs. Crosswhite is very generous," Eva concurred.

Cass regarded the relatively small serving she'd taken. "I know," she said uneasily. "There's so much food I feel guilty."

Eva inclined her head slightly, studying Cass through

amber eyes half veiled by thick lashes. "Guilty for what you take or guilty for what you leave behind?" she asked.

"Either. Both." Cass shrugged helplessly.

"There is no need. It does appear to be—what is the phrase—an embarrassment of riches. But the food does not go to waste. Every afternoon we deliver meals to the local shelter."

"I tried to help with the actual cooking myself," Emilie said cheerily, catching Cass off guard with her sudden entrance. "But Natalie and Consuela mutinied. They threw me out of my own kitchen, if you can imagine!"

"There are some things," Eva confided, "that even starving people will not eat."

"Now, Eva, we don't know for a fact no one would have eaten my corn bread. But after the pancake incident, Mark decided to err on the side of caution rather than risk all those potential dental bills. Good morning, dear," Emilie said to Cass. "I hope you slept well."

Cass was growing used to Mrs. Crosswhite's disconnected conversational style. "It's a very comfortable room," she said.

Emilie didn't notice the evasion. "Good, good. Well, I must be off." With a quick fluttery wave, she was gone.

Cass was so distracted by her hostess's sudden appearance and equally rapid exit that she almost forgot to return the locket. She caught up with Emilie by the front door. "Mrs. Crosswhite, wait! I should have given this back to you last night. I'm sorry. Thank you for letting me wear it."

Mrs. Crosswhite made no move to reclaim the antique necklace Cass held out. "Don't you like it, dear?"

"I love it. It's beautiful."

"Oh, good. I thought for a moment I might be losing

my touch. I'm usually quite clever at choosing the right gift for someone."

"Gift?" The meaning of the word penetrated slowly. Even then, Cass could scarcely believe she'd grasped Emilie's intention correctly. "This was your grandmother's locket," she began.

"So it was. And now it's yours. That locket needs some new memories. Now really, I must be going. I'll see you at lunch, dear."

Cass walked back to the breakfast room in a daze.

"Is something wrong?" Eva asked.

"Mrs. Crosswhite gave me this necklace. It belonged to her grandmother."

"That would have been Luella," Eva said, nodding. "She was wearing it the night Joseph Cushing proposed to her. Then Luella's daughter, Margaret, wore it on her own wedding day."

Cass was surprised by Eva's easy familiarity with the Crosswhite family history.

"Margaret gave it to Emilie for her sixteenth birthday," the housekeeper continued, "and Emilie was wearing it when she fell in love with Hartley Crosswhite."

Cass was stunned to discover the locket had so much personal sentiment attached to it. "It's a family heirloom," she protested. "How can Mrs. Crosswhite give something like this to a stranger?"

Eva lifted one shoulder indifferently. "This whole house is filled with heirlooms. One more or less will make no difference to Emilie. What matters is that she thinks this one is a romantic talisman. Perhaps Mrs. Crosswhite has plans for you." She gave Cass a conspiratorial grin.

Cass's cheeks warmed at the implication. To avoid Eva's knowing glance, she turned her wary gaze on the deceptively innocent-looking necklace. She mentally tallied the events Eva had listed as being associated with the locket, then added her own encounter in the garden with Gabe Preston.

It would be rude to refuse such a thoughtful and generous gift, and cowardly to reject it out of superstitious fear. No piece of jewelry could change how Gabe Preston felt about her, or how she felt about him. She ran her fingertips across the delicate engraving. She didn't really wish to change Gabe's feelings. She would settle for understanding them.

Cass sighed. It was herself she didn't understand at all lately.

Eva mistook the tenor, if not the subject, of Cass's thoughts. "You know, he's quite wealthy himself," she said familiarly.

On the verge of fastening the locket around her neck, Cass changed her mind and thrust it into her pocket. She would put it on later. "Emilie's cousin Edgar mentioned she has an art room," Cass said, changing the subject. "After breakfast would you mind showing me where it is?"

"Not at all," Eva said placidly. If Cass's failure to respond to her personal overture bothered her, there was no outward sign.

A short time later Cass was left alone in the art room. The huge airy studio, flooded with light, was lined with shelves and cabinets containing barely used art supplies of every description. Emilie had apparently tried her hand at many different media, abandoning them all after discovering she was equally unskilled at them all. Cass needed no further inducement to borrow a sketch pad and paper than Edgar's assurance the night before that Emilie would be thrilled to have her use them.

Feeling creatively energized for the first time in months,

Cass headed into the rear gardens seeking inspiration. She settled in an area that offered both marble benches and fountains, as well as an unobstructed view of the main house. Over the next few hours she changed position several times, searching out different angles from which to draw the manor. Her drawings became progressively more fanciful, too. She had transformed the lovely neoclassical house into a medieval castle, then an Italian villa, and was diligently turning it into a Gothic mansion complete with gargoyles when a young boy startled her out of her artistic reverie.

"Excuse me, miss," he said, shrinking back as though he thought Cass might strike him. He looked like a miniature version of the guard at the gate, with his high cheekbones, warm cocoa skin and mysterious amber eyes. This child's eyes were wary, however, and his manner distrustful, a distinct contrast to the self-assurance of the older man he otherwise resembled. "My sister Eva says for you to come to lunch," the boy mumbled. He backed away to a safe distance before turning and running off.

Cass didn't think of herself as particularly intimidating. Perhaps the child was simply shy around strangers. Or perhaps, she mused, women in general made him uncomfortable. He appeared to be about twelve years old, the right age to start feeling flustered around adult females.

Cass gathered up her supplies and began walking toward the house. She realized she hadn't seen Gabe Preston all day. As she moved around the grounds, she'd encountered several people industriously working on the landscaping. Gabe had not been one of them. She wished this sudden invisibility implied trust in her. More likely, he knew that within the confines of the estate, she was a captive, if a willing and pampered one.

Emilie Crosswhite sat at a table on the terrace. Four

places had been set, and a large pitcher of lemonade stood next to a fresh floral centerpiece. "Sit down, dear," Emilie prompted Cass. "I hope you're hungry. Consuela makes such a lovely crab salad. I'm famished. Talking to lawyers always has that effect on me. I'm not sure why."

Cass looked around for somewhere to put the sketchbook and pencils. "You've been working," Emilie noted. "May I see what you've done?" Cass felt self-conscious about the transformations her drawings had made on the venerable manor house. She wouldn't have felt right denying Mrs. Crosswhite, though. Maybe her hostess would only look at the top few, which were comparatively realistic.

Emilie studied the first sketch while Cass shifted nervously in her seat. She realized she cared very much what Emilie thought of her work. Cass reached for the lemonade and poured a full glass, hastily gulping down half of it as she awaited the old woman's reaction. She glanced around furtively, relieved that there was no other potential audience around.

The fact that she was at last alone with her hostess slowly filtered through her discomfort. This was the opportunity she'd been hunting for and she'd almost allowed it to slip by. She leaned forward and lowered her voice to further insure privacy. "Maybe now would be a good time for us to discuss your problem."

"What problem is that, dear?" Emilie turned the page to the next sketch.

"The household accounts," Cass reminded her.

Emilie's brow creased and she looked up in puzzlement. "Have I forgotten to pay you for something?"

Apparently any concern about internal theft had slipped Mrs. Crosswhite's mind. "You called Laughlin and Denmore," Cass said. "You were concerned about irregularities in the housekeeping books. You asked for me to come and stay here so I could perform a confidential audit."

Emilie's face relaxed. "Oh, that," she said with evident relief. "I had to have some excuse to bring you out here today. I knew you wouldn't be able to concentrate on work thinking about poor Crudley and waiting for the phone call. So I made up a story to take care of everything. I hope you don't mind?"

Cass mentally flashed on the restless hours she'd spent suspecting those near and dear to Emilie. Then she wondered what she would say to Mr. Denmore about her assignment at Crosswhite Manor and how she would explain her failure to secure any of Emilie's business for the firm. It served no purpose to dwell on any of that now. As usual Emilie had meant well. "You're very kind," she said to Emilie with complete sincerity. "Thank you."

Emilie beamed at the praise and returned her attention to the sketches. Cass sipped her lemonade, mindful of a growing empathy for Gabe and the rest of Mrs. Crosswhite's employees. Protecting the world from the consequences of Emilie's spontaneous good intentions could be a full-time job in itself.

Her hostess had reached the last of the drawings. She contemplated the uncompleted Gothic rendering the longest. Without looking at Cass she finally said, "Gabriel didn't tell me you had a talent for caricature."

Cass dared to hope Emilie was using the term loosely in reference to the stylistic revisions drawn on the house.

"I think I look perfectly lovely as a pussycat," Emilie continued, dashing Cass's brief optimism. She had obviously recognized her distinctive cherubic features on the cat sunning itself in the bottom corner of the sketch.

Cass slumped down in her chair. She shouldn't have

let Emilie see the drawings. She should never have let her imagination run wild in the first place. "I'm sorry," she mumbled, unable to meet the other woman's eye.

"Whatever for, dear? The renderings are wonderful. So imaginative! You're really very talented. You captured me completely with just a few lines. I can't say Gabriel will be equally pleased, although he does make a wickedly handsome gargoyle."

Emilie had noticed that, too! Cass felt like crawling under the table.

"I suppose it is an appropriate rendition," Emilie mused. "His job is to scare evil spirits away and protect the house. I hope he hasn't been giving you too bad a time."

Emilie's voice had softened noticeably on the last statement. Cass looked up and saw genuine concern in the woman's eyes. "No. No, he hasn't," Cass hastily assured her. It didn't matter to Cass whether or not it was precisely the truth.

Emilie looked relieved. "Good," she said, reaching for the lemonade pitcher to refill both their glasses. "He can be difficult, I know. In that way he's very like my late husband. They have their redeeming qualities, though." She tipped a wink at Cass as though they both knew what she meant.

"My Hartley was the most romantic man I ever met," Emilie reminisced. "He used to tell me that for him it was love at first sight. I see pictures of myself back then, such a pretty young thing I was, and I can see how a man might be smitten. But, oh my, I hadn't a thought in my head in those days. Some people will tell you that hasn't changed. But really, I was a callow girl, delicate and overpampered. Yet Hartley fell in love with me. He said it was the gentleness of my soul he loved. He saw it shining in my eyes."

Emilie's voice had grown wistful. Her eyes filled with memories as she spoke. Cass had no difficulty believing Hartley Crosswhite had known in an instant he would love this woman all his life.

"He must have been a very perceptive man," Cass said.

Emilie blinked and brought herself back to the present. "What a sweet thing to say. I wish you could have met him. I'm certain he would have liked you. As I say, in many ways he was quite like Gabriel."

Emilie's own revelations and her warm manner inspired confession from the usually reticent Cass. "Gabe doesn't like me very much," Cass denied. "He may be attracted to me, but he wishes he weren't. He questions my motives concerning everything I do. He doesn't believe in me."

Emilie shook her head so vigorously her white cherubic curls bounced wildly. "It isn't you he mistrusts, it's himself."

Cass looked doubtful. "That's hard to believe. He acts so sure of himself and so suspicious of me."

Emilie folded her hands on the table and peered intently at Cass. "Gabriel won't have told you much about his past. It's not my place to speak of things he deems private. I only hope you can avoid judging him too harshly for being somewhat overprotective of me. Under other circumstances, you would find his loyalty to me completely admirable, especially when it prevails despite the presence of such a compelling distraction."

Cass hadn't thought of herself or the situation in those terms before, but she wondered now about Gabe. *Did* he view her as a distraction, intentionally trying to divert him from his duties? If so, what must he think about what happened last night?

Humiliation surged through her. She dropped her eyes, unable to meet Emilie's frank gaze. Cass flinched when Emilie lightly touched her hand. "Dear? I hope I haven't distressed you. I didn't mean to imply Gabriel was hiding any shameful secrets. Here, have another sip of lemonade."

Cass didn't bother to correct Emilie's off-target analysis of her discomfort, arrived at, no doubt, by Emilie's usual leapfrog logic. It wasn't Gabe's actions, but her own that pained her. She'd been the aggressor in the garden last night, while Gabe had been the one holding back.

She drank deeply of the lemonade, trying to cool the heat of embarrassment. At that moment she hoped she never saw Gabe Preston again. If she could stay out of his way just a few hours longer, until the kidnappers made contact, she would be out of his life forever.

Warm hands dropped lightly and caressingly on her bare shoulders as if to prove that her luck was running true to form lately—all bad.

"Gabriel, darling. Sit down and have lunch with us. Eva will be out in a moment."

Trailing one finger down Cass's arm, Gabe circled the table to kiss Emilie's cheek. His eyes fell on the drawings still in front of Emilie. "Cute cat," he said. "But that one gargoyle needs a little work. He's a bit too ugly, even for a monster."

"An artist can only work with the material she's given," Emilie said breezily, winking at Cass.

"You can afford to be magnanimous," Gabe griped. "She obviously likes you."

Cass cringed inwardly. If Gabe had any doubts about the sincerity of her kisses last night, the drawing she'd made of him this morning wouldn't help. "It doesn't mean anything," Cass said feebly. "When I'm caught up in one of these fantasy drawings, all sorts of things just materialize before I know it. It's all subconscious." Her explanation began to sound worse than the original offense. Cass pressed her lips together to keep from blurting out anything else.

"He's just teasing, dear. Gabriel, sit down and behave yourself. Cass and I have enough on our minds without having to worry about you."

Gabe sprawled in one of the wrought iron chairs, his long legs stretched out in front of him. "Speaking of which," he began, a trace of a scowl narrowing his eyes, "what exactly are you two planning to do when the kidnappers call this afternoon?"

"Whatever they tell us to," Emilie piped up instantly.

"As long as it doesn't involve Mrs. Crosswhite personally. Only me," Cass added. She was determined to keep Emilie—and Gabe Preston—from any further entanglement in her problem.

Gabe sighed and shook his head slowly. "You're making a mistake."

"I want my cat back," Cass insisted.

"This isn't the best way to accomplish that. I want you to consider an alternative." Both Cass and Emilie began to protest immediately. Gabe raised one hand to silence them. "Just hear me out. I think when the kidnappers call, you should tell them exactly what happened. Explain that they snatched the wrong cat. Emilie has no interest in the one they do have. But out of simple kindness, she is willing to give them a token payment of, say, two hundred dollars in order to see that the animal is returned to its rightful owner. If they release him anywhere in Cass's neighborhood, Crudley could find his way home, couldn't he?" Gabe looked to Cass for her agreement.

Reluctantly she nodded. "But there isn't any reason for them to go to all that trouble for a couple of hundred dollars."

"She's right, Gabriel. They said they wanted ten thousand dollars."

"That was when they thought they had Princess Athabasca."

"And once we tell them they don't," Cass argued, "and that we won't pay them what they want, they'll just dump Crudley wherever they can. I'm not going to try and bargain with them."

"If they did just release him, he'd be okay. You could run an ad in the 'lost and found' section of the newspaper," Gabe said, but without much conviction.

"I'm not taking any chances. I have the money and I'm willing to pay for Crudley's return. That's the end of it."

"Then at least let me make the exchange," Gabe offered.

"No."

"It doesn't have to be you," he persisted.

"He's my cat. He's my responsibility. That's all there is to it. As long as I don't endanger Emilie, what business is it of yours?"

The challenge sounded more belligerent than she'd intended, but Gabe's continued opposition made her stomach churn with anxiety. If he somehow convinced Emilie to withdraw her cooperation, she'd be helpless to save Crudley.

Gabe's jaw tightened. His eyes narrowed further until Cass could barely see the dark fire flickering in them. "I guess you're right," he said. "What happens to you and your cat is none of my business."

"Gabriel!" Emilie scolded. "And Cass!" she added reprovingly. "You're both overwrought. Well, of course we all are with poor Crudley at the mercy of these horrid kidnappers. But we must settle down and work together. Now, Gabriel, you must stop trying to interfere with our plans. Cass knows you mean well, but she hasn't the patience to be tactful at the moment. Don't keep—"

She broke off and looked up with a big smile on her face. "Here's Eva with lunch. I'm sure she doesn't want us giving her indigestion by arguing all through the meal. And Consuela will be terribly disappointed if we don't appreciate her crab salad. Let's just relax and enjoy one another's company. Everything is going to turn out fine. You'll see."

Cass hadn't felt seven years old in a long time. A guilty peek at Gabe revealed Emilie's loving chastisement had produced some effect in him, as well. He didn't seem abashed in the slightest, but he did look subdued.

Eva joined them for lunch and thanks to Emilie's tireless good spirits and unflagging efforts, time passed fairly quickly for Cass, who'd been dreading the long wait for the kidnappers' call. After lunch Emilie insisted the four of them play mah-jongg. Cass didn't know how, so the others all tried to teach her at once. She realized almost immediately that Emilie was too scattered and Gabe to preoccupied to provide any useful instruction. Eva proved to be a natural tutor, however, if a little more competitive than the rest of the group. For a while Cass was able to lose herself in the intricacies of the game.

When the kidnappers' call came late in the afternoon, Cass, Gabe and Emilie all retreated to a large sitting room off the terrace as Eva excused herself. Emilie had put a cordless phone on every available surface it seemed, enough for a dozen people to listen in. Cass smiled at the woman's overreaction, but was pleased that her confederate took this so seriously.

Emilie's conversation with the kidnapper was slow but succinct. He gave halting instructions in muffled tones, obviously trying to disguise his voice. Emilie, glancing from Gabe's frowning face to Cass's hopeful one and back again, for the most part acceded to what he said. She got no argument about Cass acting as the go-between. After she hung up, Emilie took a deep breath and clapped her hands together in delight. "That went perfectly, don't you think?"

Cass nodded with relief. She and Emilie both looked to Gabe for confirmation. His stony expression and tensed muscles fairly screamed the predator's frustration at being excluded from the hunt.

"Gabriel?" Emilie asked tentatively.

He pushed off from the desk he'd been leaning against, turning away from them to stare out at the terrace. The rigid set of his shoulders made his silence more ominous than any argument. Cass forced herself not to echo Emilie in asking for his approval.

"Gabriel?" Emilie persisted. "Isn't this going to work out fine? The kidnappers didn't have any new demands, and they offered to make the exchange in a public place. Everything is going according to plan. There's nothing for you to worry about."

"There's plenty to worry about. I've said all along that I don't like the whole setup of this kidnapping. It doesn't make sense. Unless there's a more lucrative twist down the line, it isn't worth the risk to a professional. And if it's amateurs pulling it, then too many things can go wrong."

"Not if we follow their instructions," Cass inserted. "And that's what I intend to do."

"If that tone of voice is supposed to intimidate me,

you'll have to try something else. No, don't," Gabe said wearily, pivoting to face Cass. "I'm through trying to talk sense into either of you. It's a waste of my time and energy. As I've been frequently reminded, my judgment has no value. My feelings are irrelevant." He spun around and left through the terrace doors, disappearing into the gardens.

Gabe's abrupt and angry exit stunned Cass. Emilie hastened to her side to reassure her. "Don't worry, dear. He's just annoyed that he won't be allowed to gallop up on a white horse and rescue you. Men adore that sort of thing. I suppose we do, too, even when we're perfectly able to take care of ourselves. He'll get over it."

Cass clenched her hands into tight fists. "I'll help him," she muttered. She went in the direction he'd taken. Whenever she ran into any of the gardening staff, she asked, "Gabe Preston?" Most of them shrugged and smiled, but one or two pointed the way he'd gone. Given the size of the estate, she found him relatively rapidly. She stalked over to within a few feet of where he was working and snapped, "I don't understand what it is you think you have to be angry about."

Gabe continued digging furiously in the flower bed, burying a piece of electronic equipment. He barely paused to glare at her. "Don't you?"

Cass felt her own temper rising. "No, I don't. You said you didn't want Emilie involved. Well, as of this minute, she's out of the whole business. Nothing that happens from here on will affect her in any way."

"Is that how you see it?"

"That's how it is. Whatever happens tomorrow, she won't be hurt by it."

Gabe thrust his shovel deep into the earth and turned to face Cass. "You have a pretty shortsighted view of how human relationships operate. When you came here

Monday, you deliberately intruded into Emilie Crosswhite's life. You can't just walk away now and pretend nothing has changed for you or for her. Emilie likes you. She cares about you. How do you think she'll feel if something goes wrong tomorrow and you don't get Crudley back? How will she feel if you get hurt?" Gabe took two quick steps toward Cass, ripping off his gloves and throwing them to the ground before grabbing her by the shoulders. His voice dropped to a husky whisper. "How the hell do you think I'll feel if you get hurt?"

Heat radiated from Gabe's sun-bronzed skin, and the scent of warm earth clung to him. His sheer physical presence was almost overwhelmingly potent. Cass wanted to run from the emotions storming in his eyes, but she was caught, held by the elemental force that drew her to him despite the danger.

"I can take care of myself," Cass said, but the tremor in her voice betrayed her.

Gabe pulled her close. "Can you?" It wasn't so much a question as a dare. Without releasing her, Gabe dropped one hand down her back to her waist in a long caress that pressed her firmly against him. The fingers of his other hand twined through her hair, gently but insistently tilting her head back. His intention was clear. Cass wondered why, though, she felt a shiver of fear. It wasn't as though it would be the first time she'd kissed him. Then Gabe's lips met hers with an urgency and fierceness completely unexpected, and she felt as though she'd never been truly kissed before.

A firestorm of unforeseen sensations swept through her body. Her knees buckled, but Gabe was holding her so tightly she couldn't fall. She couldn't seem to breathe, but it didn't matter. Gabe's breath was warm on her cheek, and she was sure he was breathing for both of them.

Then they were lying on the ground somehow, Gabe's

weight pressing Cass against the fragrant grass. His fingers slid along the bare skin of her thigh. She arched against him, wanting to be closer. Gabe drew his breath in sharply and rolled onto his back, pulling Cass over on top of him. His mouth was hungry and demanding. Cass surrendered to his expertise and her own desire, acknowledging the intimacy that had grown between them, despite all her efforts to forestall it.

When he broke away from her, Cass felt it as an almost physical pain. She opened her eyes to the hot glare of sunlight. Gabe was a stark silhouette standing above her, his shadow falling across her. He bent down and lifted her effortlessly to her feet. His breathing was uneven, but not from physical exertion. "You'd better go," he said. He turned away and picked up his gloves and shovel. A moment later he resumed digging.

Cass didn't understand any part of what had just happened. Her confusion focused on the most compelling point. "You didn't kiss me like that last night," she said. It sounded like an accusation.

"Last night I was being careful not to scare you."

"Scare me?" Cass lifted her chin. "What could you possibly do that would scare me?" Given that her voice rasped unsteadily and her whole body still trembled, the question lacked the disdain Cass aimed for.

Gabe leveled an intimate stare at her that should have been answer enough. Then he said, "Don't forget I talked to a lot of people while I was investigating you. I know you aren't very worldly where men are concerned."

Cass had been upset that Gabe felt free to invade her privacy to any degree, but this was a new low for him. "You talked to people I used to date? You asked them about..." Cass could imagine the questions Gabe had asked to elicit his information, and the impression he must have left with her friends and acquaintances. "You are disgusting," she said with barely controlled fury. "You have no excuse for delving into—"

"I don't need an excuse. My justification hasn't changed. Your friends all agreed you were too honest to devise this kidnapping stunt on your own. I had to know more. I had to know if it was possible that you were being used either knowingly or unknowingly, by someone less scrupulous."

"Someone? You mean some *man?*" Cass didn't need the look on Gabe's face to confirm her deduction. She suddenly felt nauseated. A minute ago, she thought there was nothing more horrible Gabe Preston could believe about her than that she was a crook. She'd been wrong. It was worse, far worse, that he thought she was so pathetic, so desperately needy, that she could be manipulated into committing a crime by the flattering attentions of the wrong kind of man.

Cass wanted to run and hide. But she was determined now to hear all of it. "So you decided to see for yourself how naive I really am," she said. "You decided to see for yourself how easily I could be led astray by a little romance. I trust your experiments supported your foregone conclusions?"

Gabe's eyes flashed with what might have been surprise or pain, quickly hidden behind his dark lashes. The air between them shimmered with heat. "We both know the answer to that," he said softly. "I had nothing to prove, to either of us. I wasn't testing you. But maybe it's better for both of us if you believe I was. Go back to the house. You have what you wanted from Emilie. And more than you wanted from me." He walked off through a maze of hedges, leaving Cass with the uneasy feeling that she'd misjudged him again.

Chapter Nine

Saturday morning Cass sat in the breakfast room tearing a cinnamon roll into tiny pieces, only occasionally eating any. Dinner the night before had been served on a tray in her room after she pleaded a headache. Both Eva and Mrs. Crosswhite had stopped by offering sympathy and various headache remedies. Cass hadn't expected Gabe, and he'd remained pointedly absent.

Cass continued to shred her roll. She should feel elated. For the first time in nearly a week the end of her ridiculous ordeal was in sight. She had the money, the rendezvous was arranged, and Gabe had agreed not to interfere. Crudley's safe return was only hours away. Tomorrow Cass's life would return to normal. She could forget this whole awful week.

Except it hadn't been only awful, and she didn't want to forget it. She felt a sharp pain beneath her ribs whenever she thought about never again seeing any of the people she'd met at Crosswhite Manor. Everyone had been so kind to her. Even before Gabe's angry outburst yesterday, she'd realized how personally involved she'd become with Emilie Crosswhite. What she'd once envisioned as her reckless assault on a fortress of wealth and power in order to save her cat had become something else entirely. It was her own defenses that had been broken down when her preconceptions had been forced to yield to a reality far different than she'd assumed.

Gabe Preston had fared the worst because of her careless prejudgment. In the dark quiet hours of the night, she'd finally managed to see things from his perspective. He'd been honest with her throughout their brief relationship. She didn't like what he'd done, but she could see how he'd feel obligated to do no less.

She'd tried to dismiss him as a wealthy idler, amusing himself at her expense. But in truth he was nothing like that. She probably owed him an apology. She wondered if she had the courage to offer it. Maybe when Crudley was home safe and sound, her emotional equilibrium would return. Then she could make a fresh start with Gabe.

Cass took a deep breath. Nothing had to end today unless she chose to let it. She'd cut herself off from too many people in the past. She wouldn't make that mistake again.

Cass poured a glass of orange juice from a beautiful cut-glass pitcher. As she did, the facets caught the early sunlight and fractured it into dozens of tiny rainbows. Cass tilted and turned the pitcher, flinging the bright colors across the snowy white tablecloth and pale lemon walls.

"I've always loved that pitcher," Emilie announced gaily. Her noiseless approaches constantly surprised Cass, particularly given the lady's penchant for rustling silks under ruffles of chiffon. This morning's creation featured clouds of orchids in shades of lavender and blue. Emilie swirled into a chair. "My mother used to pour milk from this pitcher at breakfast. The sun streamed through our windows the way it does here, scattering rainbows everywhere, onto the dishes, into my bowl, and my mother would say, 'We're having rainbows for breakfast.' Then every evening she would ask me where that day I'd found the pot of gold. She was teaching me that each day is special if you make it so by noticing the beauty around you, or doing a kindness for someone, or accepting a favor. I hope that's not all you're having for breakfast? You're not still feeling ill, are you?"

"I'm fine," Cass assured her.

"Good! You must be strong today, you know, for Crudley's sake." Emilie leaned forward. "Now, dear," she said softly, "I want you to take this." She withdrew an envelope from the pocket of her floral gown and slid it toward Cass, glancing around the room as though checking for spies.

Cass picked up the thick pink vellum envelope and lifted the unsealed flap. Inside she saw a neat bundle of thousand-dollar bills.

"I don't want you to argue with me," Emilie began when she saw the protest form on Cass's lips. "I've given the matter a lot of thought, and poor Crudley would not be in this predicament if I weren't wealthy. But I am. There you have it. Since it's my money that caused this grief, it should be my money that alleviates it."

While Emilie spoke, Cass shook her head slowly from side to side, partly in disbelief, partly in denial. "I can't accept—"

"Please, Cass dear. Allow me to do this. I can so easily afford the ransom and you cannot."

What Emilie said was true. Ten thousand dollars might

be Cass's life savings, but it was a pittance to Emilie Crosswhite. Her would-be benefactor could make the same gesture a hundred times over without seriously impacting her net worth. So why should Cass's eyes suddenly sting and her throat tighten? She reached for her napkin. "I don't know what to say." Her words stumbled past too much emotion.

"Say you'll let me help you, dear. Let this be the favor you accept from a friend today."

That was Cass's problem, of course. The money wasn't a gesture to Emilie. It was a genuine expression of friendship, the tangible evidence of a kind heart and a loving spirit. Emilie couldn't be who she was and not give the ransom to Cass.

It would be completely pointless, even cruel, to argue with Emilie about this. "Thank you," Cass said. "I don't know what I would have done without your help this last week, Emilie. I can't begin to express my gratitude—"

Emilie interrupted, waving the word away as though it had a bad odor. "That will be enough of that, dear! I would like to meet Crudley, though. Perhaps you'll bring him by for a visit. Does he like crab salad?"

Cass suspected Emilie was more interested in cutting off her praises than in hearing about Crudley's eating habits. Still, the least Cass could do was cooperate with her hostess's wishes. "I'm not sure. I don't believe I've ever served him that."

"Well, we'll show him the menu and he can choose what he likes. That's what Princess Athabasca does. Though sometimes she will insist on ordering something not on the menu, just to be difficult." Cass tried not to picture how this might happen. "Now, I must be off. Those tiresome lawyers! No matter how much help I give them, they seem to need more." Emilie bent down and kissed Cass's cheek. "Good luck, my dear. I know everything will work out just fine."

Alone again, Cass gave up the futile attempt to eat and headed upstairs. Though the ransom exchange was still hours away, she wanted to mentally go over the plan, checking and rechecking for possible glitches.

The kidnappers had chosen noon as the time of the swap and designated Heritage Park as the location. Cass was to sit on a specified bench, placing the money next to her in a small black backpack. Emilie had provided the backpack last night and given Cass the use of one of the estate's cars for traveling to the meeting place and retrieving Crudley.

Cass had marveled at Emilie's boundless desire to be useful without seeming intrusive. And that had been before Emilie's latest beneficence. Cass sighed and stared at the pink envelope containing ten thousand dollars. Although she'd avoided any futile debate with Emilie, there was no way she could accept the money. Her character was as resolute as Emilie's. Her conscience simply couldn't bend on this point.

Cass sat at the small writing desk in her room and penned a short note thanking Emilie for her generosity and explaining why she couldn't accept. She slipped the note into the pink envelope with the bundled money and set it next to her purse, the backpack and the borrowed car keys. Then she lay down on the bed rerunning the details of the ransom exchange through her mind.

Shortly after eleven-thirty, Cass gathered up her gear and went downstairs. Gabe must have been nearby waiting for her to appear. He materialized out of nowhere as she turned toward the east wing of the house to search for Eva. With one quick appraising glance, he sized up her preparations. "Ready to go?" he asked. His voice carried no inflection of any kind. His features had assumed a completely neutral expression.

"I was just looking for Eva." Cass wanted to say more. She wanted to assure Gabe she understood his misgivings and regretted some of her behavior, which must have seemed both selfish and self-destructive. She wanted to thank him for deciding to trust her when it mattered most. And more than anything, she wanted to break down the barrier they'd erected between them. "Maybe you could give this to Emilie," she suggested, handing him the pink envelope. "It's a thank-you note."

"I'll see she gets it," Gabe said curtly. Then he turned and walked off.

Unspoken words burned in Cass's throat. Only the knowledge that Crudley needed her immediate attention kept her from rushing after Gabe. Her human relationships could wait for clarification. Right now Crudley depended on her alone.

It took Cass only a few minutes to arrive at Heritage Park. As she walked through the Saturday crowds of families and tourists, she wondered if she should have arrived earlier. The bench she was to sit on already had several other occupants. Cass squeezed onto one end with an apologetic smile to the elderly man she bumped over slightly. He smiled in return and made a little extra room for her. Cass placed the backpack on the outside edge of the bench. She pulled out a paperback book she'd brought in order to look properly inattentive when the bag with the money was swapped for one with Crudley's location in it. Cass glanced at the watch of the elderly man next to her. It was barely a quarter to twelve.

Everything happened at once after that. Cass felt, rather than saw, the backpack snatched from the bench. She glanced where it had been and saw nothing in its place.

She scanned the grass around her, convinced the replacement pouch containing Crudley's whereabouts must have fallen or been pushed to the ground. In dismay she looked up and saw the park explode into activity. One man running suddenly became half a dozen men running in all directions. A flock of gulls burst into flight. Dogs broke loose from their masters and began chasing birds and runners. Everyone was shouting, barking or cawing.

In the middle of the turmoil, Cass saw Gabe. He had an armlock on a man holding a black backpack in his hand. Cass started running, too.

She never saw the police arrive. She was pulling on Gabe's arm, trying desperately to force him to release his hold on the kidnapper, when strong hands gripped her shoulders and bodily lifted her away from the struggling pair. She fought the interference, but was nonetheless half-pulled, half-dragged back from the fight. Only then did she register the presence of at least five uniformed policemen, two of whom were helping Gabe haul the hapless kidnapper back to his feet.

One of the officers whipped a pair of handcuffs from his equipment belt. They were going to arrest the man. She would never see Crudley again. "No!" The strangled cry burst from Cass's throat as she strained against the hands still holding her.

"Easy, miss," a deep voice advised from behind her left ear. "It's all over."

Something in the calm authoritative tone of voice warned Cass that her captor wasn't simply an interfering bystander. She twisted her head to peer over her shoulder into the icy blue eyes of yet another policeman. His calculating look and the continued strength of his grip on her shoulder told her he hadn't yet decided if she was one of the good guys or one of the bad.

The officer's wariness made sense. He must have seen her wrestling with Gabe. He'd certainly heard her anguished cry at the thief's apprehension. Neither he nor any of the other policemen knew yet it was her backpack that had been stolen. And once they knew that, how would she explain her bizarre conduct without implicating the thief in the other crimes?

This was a mess. The authorities would not be likely to dismiss the burglary at the veterinary clinic and the attempted extortion from Emilie Crosswhite if the perpetrator was handed to them on a silver platter. She couldn't let that happen. Cass had to keep Gabe from telling the truth to the police.

Frantically she turned back toward the commotion, looking for Gabe. He was already striding in her direction, wearing the same look of steely-eyed determination the police all displayed. Oh, Lord. What a time for him to decide to be both heroic and righteous.

As he approached, Gabe's eyes searched Cass's face, then flicked quickly over her body, as if he needed to reassure himself she was whole and sound. Then he jerked his head at the knot of policemen still gathered around the kidnapper, trying to keep the gawking citizens from endangering themselves. "Your sergeant needs you over there," Gabe informed Cass's custodian.

The officer acknowledged the order with a nod of his head and a brisk "Yes, sir."

Cass contained herself until the officer was out of earshot, then turned on Gabe. "This is all your fault!" she hissed, trying not to attract the attention of the departing policeman. "I had everything under control. It was all going according to plan until you interfered. And you promised! Now the police are part of it, and unless you help me come up with some believable lie to explain what happened here, they're going to put that man in jail and I'll never see Crudley again."

"That's the least of your problems," Gabe advised her, anger heating his sea green eyes. "Right now you better think of a way to explain why you were helping a known felon steal ten thousand dollars."

"It's my money! He wasn't stealing it. I was giving it to him willingly."

An unreadable emotion flickered across Gabe's face before his features resumed their stony set. "It's not your money," he said quietly. "It's Emilie's. I know."

The smug reply, that Emilie had given her the money but she had returned it, died on Cass's lips. So that was why Gabe had come to the park—not to protect Cass, but to safeguard Emilie Crosswhite's investment. A stab of pain Cass attributed to injured pride killed any impulse to reveal the truth now. Let Gabe think what he wanted. It made no difference, except for emphasizing that she couldn't count on his help with the police. She was on her own.

Fine. She would have to make up some story to tell the police. She could say the thief was not a thief at all. Her backpack had been stolen by a completely different person. The supposed thief had chased the original pack-snatcher and retrieved her property, only to be mistaken for the crook by Gabe, who in turn chased down the good Samaritan to recoup her property yet again. It was flimsy. But if Cass insisted that Gabe had tackled the wrong man, a man who was only trying to be helpful, eventually the police would have to let the man go. It would be Gabe's word against hers.

Explaining why she was carrying ten thousand dollars in cash in a backpack for a trip to a public park would be tougher. Cass glared at Gabe and folded her arms across her chest as if daring him to ask her that very question. He wouldn't, of course, because he knew the real answer. To the police she would simply pose as an eccentric who had lost faith in the U.S. banking system.

"Excuse me." Cass swung around and almost bumped into one of the policemen standing nearby. He'd been watching her and Gabe, unsure about when to interrupt an obvious but nonviolent confrontation. "You'll have to come with me to the station, miss."

"Never mind, Officer Staley," Gabe said peremptorily. "I'll take her down in my car."

Staley gave the two of them another quick look, measuring the tension. "Whatever you say, Lieutenant," he acquiesced with a shrug. He turned and walked back to the other officers and their waiting prisoner.

It took a moment for the implications of his words to penetrate Cass's anger. She whirled on Gabe. "Lieutenant?" she repeated incredulously.

Gabe pressed his lips into a thin line and grimaced. "Technically speaking, I'm not a lieutenant anymore."

"Then just what are you?" Cass asked, her voice frigid with suspicion.

"Retired."

"Retired?" Cass scoffed. "At the ripe old age of what? Thirty? Thirty-five?"

Gabe shifted his weight uncomfortably. "Thirty-two. I was forced to take early retirement."

Cass barely listened to his explanation, homing in on the more critical deceptions that lay between them. "What service were you a lieutenant in before you retired? The army? The navy?"

Although he must have known this moment would come, Gabe didn't seem prepared for it. He looked around the park, at the dwindling knots of people talking and gesturing toward him and Cass or the uniformed officers escorting away their prisoner. Dogs barked, children shouted and ran, and trees rustled in the afternoon breeze. In spite of the recent commotion, it was a peaceful scene.

Cass felt her whole body go unnaturally still as she waited for Gabe's answer. He sighed heavily and ran his fingers through his hair. "I was a lieutenant in the Newport Police Department. Detective Division."

"All this time," Cass said. Her voice was so soft Gabe had to tilt his head to better catch her words. "It wasn't just Emilie giving me the money this morning. All this time you've been investigating me officially. You never stopped suspecting me. You never stopped believing I was trying to extort money from Emilie. Every word you've said, everything you've done, was to keep me under constant surveillance, away from my fellow conspirators, and to lull me into a false sense of security so you could catch me red-handed along with the rest of my gang of thieves."

An automatic protest rose in Gabe's throat, blocked by the realization there was a grain of truth in the accusations.

"You never cared about me or Crudley at all."

Gabe couldn't allow that to pass unchallenged. "That isn't true."

"I've been an idiot." Cass turned away and wiped the back of her hand across her eyes. "I've lost everything," she whispered hopelessly, beginning to walk away.

Gabe caught her upper arm in his strong fingers, then carefully relaxed his grip. "I know how you feel about me," he began.

"I doubt that very seriously." Cass shook him off.

"I told the officers I would take you down to the police station. There are reports to be filled out and signed. You'll be given a property receipt for the money. Ownership will be determined in court." Every word now was delivered with the proper brisk lack of inflection. He was a professional, doing his job.

"It doesn't matter," Cass mumbled. She continued to walk away, only allowing the gentle pressure of Gabe's hand on her arm to guide her course to his waiting car.

The trip to the police station passed in complete silence. Cass stared out the window and tried to think dispassionately about the past week and all that had happened to her. It was impossible. A turmoil of emotion colored everything, defying any rational consideration of events. The man beside her had become a stranger in the blink of an eye.

At the station Gabe took Cass to a glass-walled cubicle along one side of a room cluttered with desks and people. "Wait here," he instructed her tersely, then left, closing the door behind him. Cass disinterestedly checked out her surroundings. She'd been left in someone's office. Papers littered the scarred wooden desk in the center of the room. Books crowded a narrow bookcase in one corner. On the walls hung framed diplomas, commendations and awards, and pictures—all presumably meaningful to the usual occupant of the office, Sergeant Nathan Weathers, whose gold nameplate faced Cass on the desk.

Time crawled as Cass waited in lonely isolation, watching the comings and goings of people in the big room beyond the glass enclosure. She thought she recognized one of the officers who came in, sat down at an unoccupied desk and began typing a report. He looked like one of the policemen from the park.

Where was everyone else? Where was Gabe? Where was the kidnapper? Why didn't anyone come to take her statement or read Cass her Miranda rights? She wondered if she should refuse to say anything until she spoke to an attorney. So far, she hadn't committed any actual crime. At least she didn't think she had.

With each passing minute it seemed more unlikely that the kidnapper would be freed, no matter what story Cass invented to exonerate him. Lieutenant Preston—retired Lieutenant Preston—formerly of the Newport Police Department, would already have told his colleagues his own version of the truth. Anything Cass said to contradict him might lead to charges against her lying to the police or filing a false report. Those *were* crimes. She closed her eyes and leaned her forehead on the cool glass window.

The opening of the office door jarred her back to the present. Gabe stood framed in the entrance. "Let's go," he said, motioning her to follow him. Cass squared her shoulders and tried to project an air of calm composure. As she trailed Gabe, she steeled herself for the interrogation she knew must be coming. You've done nothing wrong, she reminded herself for the hundredth time. Regardless of what Gabe or the other police officers think, you've committed no crime. It isn't against the law to offer or pay a reward for the recovery of a lost pet. That's all you've been doing.

After navigating a series of crisscrossing corridors, they emerged into the parking lot outside the police station. Bright sunlight still shimmered off the shiny patrol cars, despite Cass's feeling that it should have been long after nightfall by now. Gabe strode over to his car and opened the passenger door. Cass moved a few steps away. "Let's go," he repeated tersely.

"Not until you tell me where we're going."

Gabe scowled. "Home. Emilie's. The grocery store. Wherever you want to go. Anywhere but here. Personally I'm a little tired of the place."

"You mean I'm free?"

"You were never under arrest."

"I didn't exactly volunteer to sit in that office for all those hours or to come to this police station in the first place."

Gabe sighed heavily. "You were a witness to a crime. A victim of a crime."

"A suspected accessory to a crime," Cass added.

"The situation was a little confusing. The police detained everyone they thought might be able to help in the investigation. If you had insisted on leaving, no one would have stopped you."

"How fortunate for them I didn't realize that," Cass observed.

"I told them I was sure you understood your rights. If you want to sue someone, it will have to be me."

"I don't want to sue anyone! I want to know what in the world is going on here!"

"I'm trying to take you home. Now will you get in the car?"

"Not until you tell me what's happened. Is that man under arrest? Where's my cat?"

"Yes and I don't know. If you want more explanation than that, then please get in the car. I'll tell you everything I know, but I'd prefer not to do it standing in the middle of a hot parking lot where anyone and everyone in a blue uniform can overhear us."

Reluctantly Cass agreed with Gabe's reasoning. It was unbearably hot standing on the blacktop lot, and they'd already drawn interested stares from at least two passing officers. Cass walked to the car and got in.

"Thank you," Gabe muttered with barely concealed exasperation. He began driving in the general direction of Cass's carriage-house apartment.

"I won't testify against him," Cass said, folding her

arms to project the appropriate body language. She wondered even as she said it whether when the time came she could make good on the bluff and flout the law.

"You don't have to testify against him. He's already signed a confession and the district attorney's office has agreed to a plea bargain. It's all over but the paperwork. And he never had Crudley."

There was too much information in too few words for Cass to absorb any but the most important fact. "What do you mean he never had Crudley?"

"Jimmy Tanner, the man who stole your backpack, is a small-time thief. Till-taps, snatch-and-grabs, prowling unlocked cars—those are his specialties. Nothing violent, nothing big. He was in the park, hoping to find some careless person leaving his or her valuables unattended. That's what he found all right. There you sat, reading a book, with your backpack sitting a foot away from you, completely unguarded. It's not the sort of thing Jimmy could pass up. Unfortunately for him, I know Jimmy. He and I go way back. Jimmy goes way back with almost every officer on the force. When I saw him grab your pack, I knew he was just taking advantage of an unforeseen opportunity."

"He didn't kidnap Crudley?"

Gabe shook his head. "Jimmy can't plan what he's having for dinner tomorrow. His mind doesn't work that way. He could never set up something like this kidnap-extortion scheme. Simple as it is, it's beyond him."

"So where is my cat?" Cass was thinking out loud, not really expecting a response.

"Whoever had him still has him, I suppose," Gabe answered.

Musing on the unlikely turn events had taken, Cass said, "Then I can still get him back." Her mind leaped ahead, already beginning to formulate a new plan. She would tell the kidnappers a real thief, a pack-snatcher, had upset their scheduled money drop. They could arrange a new time and place for the exchange. Cass looked over at Gabe, intending to ask him how soon the police would return her money. His dark expression stopped her in mid-thought.

Gabe pulled at the neck of his T-shirt as if it had become tight in the last few seconds. He cleared his throat noisily and drummed his fingers on the steering wheel. "I wouldn't count on hearing from the kidnappers again. Tanner pulled his little stunt fairly close to the scheduled exchange time. The kidnappers were probably already there and watching. They would have seen the whole thing, including the instantaneous arrival of lots of police. They'll know that someone had notified the authorities about this caper."

"But I didn't." Hot tears flooded Cass's eyes as she realized her only chance of recovering Crudley might have vanished. "This is a mess!" she said, slumping back against the seat.

"I know. I'm truly sorry."

"Why?" Cass asked bitterly. "You have what you wanted. Emilie didn't lose a cent of her precious money and you caught a thief. You're a hero."

"Is that what you think?" Gabe's voice was soft, yet so clearly edged with sadness that Cass couldn't answer. She turned her head and stared out the window. "I don't know your definition of a hero," Gabe continued, "but in my book, it isn't the guy who fouls up the rescue so he doesn't save the victim or get the girl in the end. Whether you believe it or not, it was just as important for me as it was for you that all this work out right. I'll be second-guessing myself about the way I handled it for a long time."

The way Gabe spoke the simple words made Cass believe him. Her breath tightened in her chest. For a moment, she wanted to be able to reassure him or forgive him, to offer him the kind of understanding he'd once offered her. But releasing her natural compassion or any of the other emotions competing for expression would make her vulnerable in a way she couldn't permit right now. She was barely holding on as it was. Only years of disciplining herself not to speak, not to reveal but to conceal her thoughts, kept her from reaching out to him, to share their mutual disappointment and pain. She didn't want that. She didn't want the barriers dissolved between them ever again. It would be too easy to depend on him, to believe in the quiet strength of purpose that radiated from him even now, to forget that he had deceived her for the entire time he'd known her.

Gabe pulled into Cass's driveway and parked the car. Before he'd shut off the engine, Cass was out and halfway up the stairs to her apartment. Cursing under his breath, Gabe followed, taking the steps two at a time with long strides that brought him to the door while Cass still fumbled with her keys. He placed one hand over hers where it rested on the doorknob. His other hand cupped her chin and tilted her face up to his. "I want to see you again," he said.

Cass couldn't believe her ears. Her stomach roiled with every turbulent emotion Gabe had provoked. "I can't," she said, pulling away from him. "There isn't any point."

"I think there is. What's happened between us these last few days, what we've felt for each other, is real. We both know that. Now may not be the ideal time to bring it up, but then, this hasn't been an ideal courtship."

"This hasn't been any kind of a courtship. It's been a surveillance." Cass backed up until her spine pressed against the wooden railing of the porch. "Ever since we met, up to and including this very instant, you've believed that I'm a crook."

"I *never* believed it. That's been my problem." Gabe ran his hand through his hair, tumbling it over his dark eyebrows where they drew together in a frown. "Look, I could spend the rest of my life explaining to you how I got to where I was mentally when I met you. I'll give you just the highlights, though. I was a reasonably good cop until I started relying too much on my personal feelings. I made one really bad mistake, and an innocent person suffered because of it. I was forced to resign."

Gabe placed his hands lightly on Cass's shoulders and felt her stiffen in response. Sighing, he released her again. "Don't you understand? I didn't trust what I felt about you. I couldn't trust it. Last time I made the mistake of relying on my instincts, people got hurt. I couldn't allow that to happen again. I had to be sure. I had to go by the book and investigate every possibility. That's what I told myself. But I couldn't stick to it. I kept fouling up at every turn, believing in you because I wanted to, instead of concentrating on all the holes in your ridiculous story. You have to admit," he said gently, "some of the things you've done haven't helped your case."

"Why should I have to prove myself to you?" Cass asked defiantly. "I never asked you for anything, except to leave me alone so I could rescue my cat."

Cass had closed down the lines of communication. Gabe knew a lost cause when he saw one. "Fine," he said wearily. "The department will contact you about reclaiming your backpack. And I'm sure Emilie will call you if she hears from the kidnappers again." For a moment, Gabe looked as though he had something else to say, but with a quick shake of his head, he turned and trudged back down the steps.

Cass opened the door and slipped into the apartment, shutting herself in her own private sanctuary. She waited for the old feelings of solitude and security to envelop her. Instead, she felt only loneliness and uncertainty. As she gazed around the room, taking in the sight of each precious and meaningful object, for the first time she could recall their familiarity gave her no comfort. The room seemed empty in a way she couldn't explain, until her imagination painted the image of Gabe sprawled on her sofa, and her memory conjured up the sound of his laughter echoing through the rooms of her apartment.

Cass rushed to the television and flipped it on, hoping its artificial brightness would fill the void. She sat in front of the screen unseeing as the darkness gathered outside her windows. Shortly before dawn, she finally slept.

Chapter Ten

When her alarm clock buzzed Monday morning, Cass seriously considered knocking it to the floor. The little bit of sleep she'd managed had been restless and troubled. Fortunately, Laughlin and Denmore didn't require smiling cheerfulness of its accountants. Even so, the prospect of spending another deadly dull day in the confines of her office overwhelmed Cass with inertia. She lay in bed contemplating calling in sick, wondering if her state of mind qualified her.

The minutes ticked by. Cass glanced at the clock. She would have to call in to say she'd be late if she decided to go to work at all. She was staring at the phone irresolutely when it began ringing. Her first impulse was to ignore it, as she had the clock. She quickly realized, however, that the call might be about Crudley. She snatched the receiver from its cradle. "Hello?" she said hopefully.

Her optimism flared when the caller identified himself as Sergeant Weathers. But while his news was not unwelcome, it was not what Cass yearned to hear. The department was prepared to release her money. She could come down to the station any time to reclaim it.

Cass disconsolately hung up the phone. At least the momentary excitement had dispelled her lethargy. And now she had a good excuse for being late. She dialed her office. "Annie," she said to her secretary's voice mail, "I'll be a little late today. I'm assisting a police investigation involving Emilie Crosswhite." That should silence any complaints about her tardiness, Cass reasoned. She regretted that Annie wasn't a gossip. Wouldn't the hushed halls of Laughlin and Denmore reverberate with a tidbit like that!

At the police station, Cass found her way back to Sergeant Weathers's office. This time, the cubicle was occupied by the man whose nameplate sat partially buried underneath stacks of reports. He stood up and extended his hand. "Miss Appleton. I'm Sergeant Weathers."

He had a warm melodic voice that had probably convinced more than one criminal to confide in him. He gestured toward an empty chair. "Please have a seat while I finish filling out these forms. Then I'll go to the property room and retrieve your money for you." He worked in silence for a minute or two. As he laid aside one piece of paper and reached for the next, he glanced up at her. "I'm sorry about your cat."

"Really," Cass said, too tired and emotionally brittle to be polite. "When I came here asking for help, no one could be bothered. Why should you care now?"

Sergeant Weathers's voice never wavered from its gentle evenness. "There was a woman in that chair half an hour ago, crying because her son committed an armed robbery. I couldn't do anything for her, either. That doesn't mean I don't feel bad about it."

His quiet words stung. Cass knew she was being unfair.

"I apologize. I guess I'm not feeling very charitable toward any of the Newport Police right now."

He stopped writing and gazed at her above the rims of his half glasses. "I hope that sentiment doesn't extend to former members of the department. Gabe Preston called in a lot of favors to bring us in on your problem." When Cass didn't answer, he added, "Gabe is one of the good guys."

This was not a topic Cass wanted to discuss with anyone, particularly one of Gabe's old friends. "I'm sure that's why he was fired," she said abruptly, hoping to dispel any notion she was personally interested in the man.

"Fired? Is that what Gabe told you?"

Cass shrugged. "He said forced to resign. It's the same thing."

"Not in this case. The only one who forced Gabe Preston to resign was Gabe Preston."

"It really isn't any of my business," Cass said, although her curiosity was slightly piqued.

"You might be surprised how much your business it is," the sergeant contradicted. "You see, a couple of years back, a woman came into Gabe's office saying she was in terrible trouble. She worked in a bank, and had just discovered that her boss had embezzled millions of dollars. What was worse, she said, was that he'd set things up so that if the theft were discovered, she would look like the guilty party. The woman was horrified to realize she could be sent to jail."

Weathers looked Cass over as if comparing her to the woman he was remembering. "She was one of those fragile helpless-looking women who bring out any man's protective urges," he continued. "Gabe, like most good cops, has a bit of the heroic streak that makes him want to rescue people. The difference in his case is that Gabe's streak is a mile wide. He needs to help people as much as he needs to breathe and eat and sleep. It's his nature."

The sergeant dropped his eyes to the papers in front of him and signed several with a quick flourish. "Naturally, Gabe began investigating the woman's story. Everything checked out, including the existence of a not very subtle trail obviously created to throw suspicion in her direction.

"In due course, her boss was arrested. So much money was missing that he was judged a flight risk and held in jail for months pending his trial."

Weathers flipped the forms around so they faced Cass. "Sign here," he said, pointing. Cass did as she was instructed, torn between wanting to leave immediately and wanting to hear the rest of the story.

"All during that time, Gabe worked closely with this woman to develop the prosecution's case. He relied on her to lead him through the fancy footwork of international banking maneuvers that camouflaged where the money had gone. She relied on him for moral strength and support, and protection against the vague threats the banker issued while protesting his innocence.

"Ultimately, the man was convicted and sentenced to prison. By that time, Gabe had decided he was in love with the woman. They became engaged and began planning their wedding. A few months later, the woman backed out of it. She told Gabe that she simply couldn't get past the awful incident that had brought them together. As long as she stayed with him, she would never be free of the terrible memories. She packed up everything she owned and left town."

Cass sank back into her chair, feeling cheated by the apparent end of Sergeant Weathers's story. Did he really think his tale of broken romance would make Cass reconsider her opinion of Gabe Preston? After all that he'd done to her, Cass wasn't about to feel sorry for Gabe. "I'm sure it was hard on him," she said grudgingly. "May I have my money back now? I'm already late for work."

Weathers lifted one shoulder and smiled obligingly. "Sorry. I thought you might want to hear the end of the story."

Cass wasn't at all sure she did. But she was convinced she would never make it through the red tape necessary to recover her ten thousand dollars without this man's cooperation. "Excuse me. I thought you had finished. Please go on," she said with careful politeness.

The sergeant appeared not to notice her impatience. "You're right about it being hard on Gabe," he said as if there'd been no interruption. "He went through the usual depression that follows a breakup, brooding and replaying his memories of their time together, trying to figure out what he should have done differently and where he went wrong. And a funny thing happened. The more emotional distance he gained from the relationship, the more clearly he saw the events that had drawn them into it. He began to notice little inconsistencies in the stories the woman had told him. Then he began to wonder how she became so knowledgeable about money-laundering schemes. And he began to suspect that the reason he'd never found the stolen money was that she'd led him carefully, step-by-step, away from where she had it hidden."

Cass understood finally why Sergeant Weathers had told her the story. Against her will, she felt a stab of sympathy for Gabe Preston. His principles were chiseled in stone. He would never forgive himself for having been misled into betraying them. "He went after her, didn't he?" Cass couldn't stop herself from asking.

Weathers smiled sadly. His expression said there were

no possible happy endings to this tale. "Gabe worked like a dog to set things right—sixteen, twenty hours a day for weeks on end. Eventually the banker was released pending a retrial, and warrants were issued for the woman's arrest. The day Interpol notified us she was in custody, Gabe resigned."

"He didn't have to do that," Cass whispered, knowing that he did.

"An innocent man spent almost two years in prison. Gabe was in charge of the investigation that put him there. Gabe thinks he should have been more skeptical. He's afraid he let personal feelings cloud his judgment."

"Is that what other people think?"

"I think she was one clever little witch. If anyone but Gabe had handled the case, it would have stayed closed for good with her in the clear. Choosing him for her mark was the only mistake she made."

Weathers rounded the desk and scooped up the papers he'd had Cass sign. "I'll be right back with your money," he said.

He shut the office door, leaving Cass alone with only her troubled thoughts for company. She understood now why Gabe hadn't wanted to talk about his former job or why he'd left it. He believed he'd failed the people who counted on him, both civilians and police. He thought his flawed judgment had caused an innocent man to be punished, although apparently none of his peers felt the same. She'd seen the respect with which he had been treated by the other officers at the park, but the implications hadn't sunk in. As far as his former co-workers were concerned, Gabe was still "one of the good guys."

Couldn't Gabe see, as his friend Sergeant Weathers did, that any fault lay completely with the woman who'd devised the treacherous embezzlement plan?

Cass slumped down in her chair, fully aware for the first time of the dilemma she'd presented to Gabe and how little she'd done to ease his predicament. While Gabe had been investigating her, trying to learn as much as he could about the kind of person she was, she had been looking for ways to use him or get around him. She had never considered that he brought his own history with him, or that his entanglement in what she thought of as her personal problem could have significant consequences for him, too.

Sergeant Weathers opened the door and reentered his office. He handed Cass a bulky manila envelope. "Please count the money before you sign the receipt," he advised.

Cass shook her head in refusal and quickly grabbed a pen to complete the transaction. She wanted to escape. The sergeant blocked her path. "Gabe and I were partners for a lot of years. We're still friends. No one knows him better than I do. Being a police officer was the most important thing in Gabe's life. He had to buck his family's disapproval and the attitudes of a lot of guys on the force who didn't know him but figured he was too rich to be serious about his job. Giving up his badge was like ripping out his heart."

Weathers took off his glasses. His dark eyes bored into Cass's as though he could see into her soul. Cass almost pitied the crooks who had to endure that kind of scrutiny. "Gabe has changed," he said quietly. "He's lost confidence in himself. He needs to be right about you. Don't disappoint him."

Cass turned away and stepped around the sergeant, toward the open door and freedom. She drove to work in a haze of self-doubt and recrimination. If she had been more cooperative and less hostile to Gabe from the start, would he have been more forthcoming about himself? If she had understood his feelings and trusted his motives, would she have followed his advice? She'd been so sure she had only herself to rely on, when she might have had him to rely on, too. They might have had each other. Crudley might be home safe now.

Cass didn't have any answers, but the questions she had convinced her she needed to take a new perspective on things. After stopping at the bank long enough to deposit her money, she drove uneagerly to work. She pulled into her parking space at the farthest end of the lot and contemplated her office building as if seeing it for the first time.

The solid brick walls and tiny windows presented the appropriate image for the stifling atmosphere and the stuffy tenants. Cass wanted to turn around and drive away, never looking back. She turned off her engine and counseled herself not to make rash decisions at this point in her life.

"You look lousy," Annie greeted Cass. "No offense."

Cass grimaced. "No offense taken." She picked up the small stack of messages and mail that had accumulated during her absence and walked into her office. She closed the door behind her and sank into her chair, leaning back and shutting her eyes.

Annie was thirty seconds behind her, entering after a brisk knock to hand Cass the unasked-for coffee. "Want to talk about it?" she inquired.

Cass shook her head. "It's a long story."

"I've got plenty of time. My boss acts tough, but she's really a nice person. I know she wouldn't object to my slacking off the work for a little while if I had a good reason. Helping a friend is a good reason, don't you think?"

Cass opened her eyes and looked at Annie in amazement. "I think you give your boss too much credit. My experience with her has been that she's kind of a jerk."

"Maybe you don't know her as well as you think you do."

"That seems to be the majority opinion lately."

"Which?" Annie teased. "That you're a jerk, or that you don't know yourself as well as you think?"

"A combination of the two, I guess."

"Is that why you look like you haven't slept all weekend? Too much soul-searching?"

"Soul-searching and lost-cat-searching—both equally unsuccessful, by the way."

"Crudley ran off?" Annie's voice was instantly filled with concern.

"Not exactly," Cass hedged. At the prospect of avoiding the subject she had indiscreetly raised herself, Cass suddenly realized how tired she was. More than tired—bone weary and mentally exhausted. The inner fortress that protected her emotional stability had been buffeted constantly from every direction for the past week. She no longer had the strength or the desire to keep all her feelings walled up, equally inaccessible to those who might try to exploit her weaknesses and those who might offer comfort and advice.

Cass saw nothing threatening in Annie's warm eyes. Would the world really end if she confided in her? Did she even care any more if it did? Gabe had been right about that much. She'd cut herself off from too many of her former friends and had avoided making new ones. She'd worried what the senior partners would think if she had a personal relationship with a subordinate.

But Annie was the best perk her job offered. Her assistant's day-in, day-out cheerfulness, her competence and her easy way with people made Cass's job tolerable.

Without Annie's presence, the weight of the stuffy old-boys-club atmosphere would long since have smothered her. Without Annie's almost invisible intervention, she would never have survived the internal political intrigues and backbiting that ran like a constant undercurrent beneath the placid surface of professionalism at Laughlin and Denmore. How could she have been so blind for so long?

"Crudley was kidnapped," Cass told Annie, prepared to reveal the whole story at the slightest sign of encouragement.

Annie gasped in dismay and reached out to lightly touch Cass's arm. "Oh, no! How horrible! Why would anyone kidnap your cat?"

Cass told her, beginning with the visit to the veterinarian's to pick up Crudley and ending with the aborted ransom drop and Gabe's deception. Annie listened to it all with an intelligent attentive expression on her face. When Cass completed her recitation, Annie sat back and sighed, collecting her thoughts. Then she leaned toward Cass and rested her forearms on the desk.

"Well," she said, "which do you want first? The advice about Crudley or the advice about Gabe?"

Cass pressed her lips tightly together. She hadn't meant to expose so much of her brief but intense relationship with Gabe Preston. The topic was impossible to avoid, however, tangled as it was from start to finish with her attempt to rescue Crudley. "The second subject is hopeless," she avowed. She could hardly deny to herself or Annie the emotional complications Gabe's intervention had created. "Say something about Crudley that will make me feel that isn't a lost cause, too."

"That's easy. You said you couldn't call Mrs. Crosswhite to make an appointment with her because she has an unlisted number, right?"

"Right."

"But the kidnappers called her on the phone." Annie watched the light dawn in Cass's eyes.

"The kidnapper has to be someone who knows Emilie's phone number," Cass concluded, then frowned. "None of her friends would kidnap Emilie's cat."

"Not for ten thousand dollars," Annie agreed.

"It would have to be someone who comes into professional contact with her. Someone who works for her, like a caterer or a delivery service."

"Don't overlook the obvious. It could be one of her own employees."

Cass shook her head in emphatic denial. "You don't know her employees. They're very well treated and fiercely protective. They seem genuinely fond of her, and with good reason. I can't imagine any of them taking vicious advantage of Emilie."

"Someone did. Someone who is not rich, who has access to Mrs. Crosswhite's personal phone number, and who knew when and where her cat would be vulnerable to kidnapping."

"I know." Cass wearily brushed her bangs from her forehead. "I'd rather think one of her employees inadvertently said too much around the wrong person."

"That's another possibility."

"One of a few too many. Still, it is a lead. I suppose I should tell the police."

"Not Gabe?"

Cass nervously straightened a loose paper clip. "He told me he isn't part of the official investigation. Besides, I don't know how to act around him after everything that's happened."

"Then maybe you're ready for part two of my advice."

"I'm afraid I'm beyond advice or help of any sort. The whole situation is hopeless. We're completely unsuited to each other. It's been an impossible relationship from the very start."

"Then it *must* be love," Annie said simply.

Cass didn't bother to deny it. She could list a dozen reasons she shouldn't have fallen in love with Gabe Preston and an equal number of arguments why any relationship with him would never work. But she'd stopped operating on logic the first time she met him, and instinct had propelled her down the short fast slide to emotional chaos from which there seemed no possible escape. "Love doesn't conquer all, though," was the only thing Cass could say now.

"Sure it does," Annie insisted, "as long as you help it out with hard work, the desire to grow, the ability to change for the better, the compassion to forgive and the thousand other things that are as much a part of love as the fact that your knees wobble every time you see him and your eyes twinkle when you say his name."

Cass groaned. "Am I that obvious?"

"To me you are, because I know you pretty well. And because I care about you."

"I haven't given you much reason to feel that way. I don't deserve a friend like you."

"I could say I don't deserve one like you. In a dozen ways every single day, you treat me like a valuable person whose feelings and opinions matter. Do you really believe most of the other accountants in this firm would make the kind of accommodations for me that you do? Do you really think this is a typical boss-secretary relationship?"

Cass smiled crookedly, trying to keep back the tears stinging her eyes. "I tried to make it one."

"You did a crummy job. You're a joy to work with. If this place didn't make you so unhappy, I'd wish you would stay forever."

"Are you telling me to quit, too?"

"Someone else has suggested it already?"

"Gabe Preston."

"He's even smarter than I thought. Don't let him get away."

"I'm not sure it's my choice at this point. I've made too many mistakes."

"None that can't be set right. Cass, he's a former police officer. He's used to dealing with upset people. He's not going to rush to a negative judgment. I'm sure you behaved at least as well as anyone else would have under the same circumstances."

Cass raised one eyebrow skeptically.

Annie wasn't deterred. "Look at it this way," she suggested. "He's seen you at your worst and he still likes you."

Cass had to laugh. "When I quit, will you come with me?"

"I can't. Who would feed and burp these big babies if I left? You'll just have to take me out to lunch sometimes and invite me to all your parties if you want to see me. Now call Gabe and tell him what you've figured out so he can help you find Crudley. The poor cat wants to come home."

Cass didn't call Gabe, though. She called Sergeant Weathers. He expressed interest, but reminded her how many people must have worked for Mrs. Crosswhite over the years, learning both her phone number and the household routines.

Next, Cass called the newspapers. She scheduled a classified ad to run for a month, offering a substantial reward, no questions asked, for the return of her lost cat. If the bungled ransom exchange had spooked the kidnappers and they dumped Crudley, someone else might find him.

Cass felt energized and in control. She dug into her work with a zeal she hadn't felt in longer than she could remember. Unfortunately, her zest subsided quickly when faced with column after column of figures.

She stared at the neat precise numbers. Why in the world had she chosen accounting as a career? She knew the answer, of course—security, stability and a certain amount of respect that attaches to people who are responsible and useful members of society. The benefits hadn't changed in the past week, but Cass's view of them had. After all, people in prison had security and stability. If they lacked respect, it was because they had misused their natural skills and abilities and applied themselves to learning the wrong things. By that definition, she belonged in jail herself. She looked around her sterile unornamented office. She was already in a cell.

Weathers called the next morning with a progress report or, more accurately, a lack-of-progress report. Cass called him Wednesday, Thursday and Friday and received the same news.

Friday evening, Cass was brooding in her apartment when the doorbell rang. She couldn't imagine who it would be, but in the fraction of a second before she opened the door, she allowed herself to think it might be the police returning her cat or Gabe giving her another chance. It was both.

The first thing Cass saw was Gabe's tall athletic silhouette, backlit by the setting sun and dappled in evening shadows. As her vision adjusted to the contrast, she noticed what Gabe held in his arms.

"Crudley," Cass whispered. Tears instantly welled up

in her eyes and spilled down her cheeks. She didn't bother to brush them away.

"Mrrow," the kidnap victim answered calmly.

Gabe tenderly passed her cat to Cass, who cuddled the animal so hard that he made a small grumble of his purr. Cass looked at Gabe with more gratitude than she'd ever felt for anyone. "How did you find him?" she asked hoarsely. Her voice wasn't working very well.

"It wasn't as easy as it should have been. First, I had to convince myself he'd really been kidnapped. By that time, the situation had developed some unexpected complications. Would you consider inviting me in for a minute?"

"Of course." Cass blushed and backed away from the doorway, allowing Gabe to enter.

He walked over to the kitchen counter and leaned against it with casual familiarity. "I assumed from the beginning that one of the estate staff had to be involved," he explained. "And I determined pretty quickly that Eva was the culprit. Someone else had to be helping her, though. It turns out she was using her little brother, Peter, as an accomplice. As terrible as that is, from my point of view the other possibilities had been even worse.

"For a while, I was afraid Eva's older brother, Paul, might be involved. He's my assistant and guards the gate, and I've always considered him a good man and a friend. Fortunately, he never had anything to do with Eva's scheme. He's pretty devastated by it, anyway. He keeps insisting that family honor demands he resign from his job. I hope I can talk him out of it. I know how he feels and I know quitting isn't the answer."

Cass heard the assurance in Gabe's voice and knew that in some way Crudley's kidnapping had given Gabe the chance to heal himself.

"My other big concern," Gabe continued, "was whether you were in on the plan."

"I didn't even know Eva until after Crudley was taken. How could I have been in cahoots with her?"

"You went to night school with her."

"I did not!"

"As a matter of fact, you did. Even though you weren't in the same classes, you were on campus at the same time two nights a week for over three months. You could easily have met."

"But we didn't."

"I know that now. You have to remember, you don't live in New York City. People here have all kinds of connections to each other they don't even realize. Did you know that you take your car to a garage where the son of one of Emilie's employees works? Or that Emilie's cook's brother is the chef at one of your favorite restaurants?"

"Stop! This is becoming more obscure and devious than the plot of most soap operas."

"I'm only trying to show you how difficult it was to clear you of any conceivable participation in the extortion."

"I believe you. And—" Cass took a deep breath, holding tightly to Crudley "—I understand."

Emotion more intense than simple relief flared in Gabe's eyes and tightened the muscles in his jaw. "I didn't blame you for accepting the ransom money from Emilie," he offered. "She had explained to me what she was going to do and why. I didn't try to stop her. When I discovered you didn't keep the ten thousand dollars, in fact, never intended to, I knew I'd been right about you all along. I wanted to tell you that before now, but I was afraid you wouldn't listen unless I brought Crudley home, too."

"I'm listening now," Cass said softly.

"I hope so. Because you have some important choices to make. For the first, and maybe the last time in your life, anything is not only possible, it's guaranteed. Emilie Crosswhite will give you whatever you ask for. If you want a partnership at Laughlin and Denmore, she'll arrange it. If you want to start your own accounting firm, she'll back you. If you want to own an art gallery, she'll build one. All you have to do is decide what matters."

Gabe pushed away from the counter and walked toward her. "What kind of security do you want, Cass? Is it the kind you've been fighting for at Laughlin and Denmore? Is it a solid bank account, a big house, a new car every year and designer clothes? Or is it the kind you can find with me—the security of knowing that I love you and I'll stand by you regardless of what happens. What do you want to count on, Cass? People or things?"

Cass read the uncertainty in Gabe's eyes and she ached to ease his doubts. "I already made my choice." She released her cat and walked to meet Gabe. "I spent every cent I have in the world to rescue my oldest friend, Crudley. I swallowed my pride to ask my new friend, Emilie, to help me. Because I knew, in my heart, that my best friend, Gabe, would see to it everything turned out right." She reached up and stroked Gabe's cheek lightly and softly kissed the corner of his mouth.

A fierce longing coupled with a passionate tenderness threatened to overwhelm Gabe's control. "I don't think I'll settle for 'best friend.'"

"How about best friend, partner and lover?"

"How about husband and father of your children?"

"One step at a time," Cass said, laughter bubbling up from a place so deep inside her she'd forgotten it existed.

"Do I get to choose which step we take next?" Gabe

asked. A slow wicked grin built into a killer smile as his hands slid around Cass's waist.

"As long as you're careful not to scare me," Cass said, using Gabe's own words from the garden to tease him now.

"What could I possibly do that would scare you?" Gabe answered. He pulled her closer.

"Everything you make me feel scares me," Cass said truthfully. Her blood was singing in her veins and she felt light-headed enough to float away like a dandelion puff. Only Gabe's steady presence and his gentle but firm embrace kept her tethered to the reality of the moment. The warm circle of his arms was all the shelter she would ever need, and his kiss promised the greatest security she had ever known, the security of being loved.

Later as they sat snuggled together, Cass found a place to begin talking. "I never thanked you for finding Crudley."

"I had no choice. I knew you would never marry me if I didn't."

Cass held up her hand, admiring the engagement ring Gabe had produced at one point from his pocket. "I might have," she said.

"Now you tell me. I suppose I should let you go on admiring my detecting skills, but actually your friend Bobby is the one who found Crudley."

"Bobby? From the clinic?"

"Yep. You see, Peter didn't know Crudley was an escape artist. He put your cat in a cage in one of the basements and left him there overnight. The next day, the Amazing Vanishing Feline was gone. By the time we had gotten around to botching the ransom exchange, Crudley had long since scampered. Peter was going to take the money, anyway, and stiff us."

"But how did Bobby get dragged in?"

"I enlisted him as a special consultant. I figured out on Monday that Peter was the guilty party, and he'd confessed to everything. By then, Crudley had been gone over a week. I checked with the rest of the outdoor staff and all the kids living on the estate. No one had seen a stray cat. I figured Crudley was gone for good. Then just as a final long shot, I checked with Bobby to see if Crudley has any bad habits that might tell us where to look next."

"You should have checked with me."

"I didn't want to get your hopes up. I really didn't think we'd find him. But that Bobby is a crafty one, and he knows Crudley. We set up the trap and Crudley walked right in. He was still on the estate grounds, actually."

"Which of Crudley's vices did you use to catch him?"

"I'd rather not say. That's confidential information, part of a police investigation. Very hush-hush."

Cass sat up straight to give Gabe the full effect of her disbelief. "Two guys with a can of tuna staking out a birdbath is hardly a top secret operation," she said.

"Mock me, if you must. Just remember, my superior investigative skills and subtle surveillance technique are all that stand between us and the dissolute life of the wealthy and unemployed now that you've quit your job."

"You know?"

"Emilie told me. She knows all the important gossip. And I want you to know I don't hold it against you that you're marrying me for my money."

"I'm marrying you *despite* your money. I'm marrying you for an entirely different set of benefits."

"Would you like me to demonstrate the full range of what I offer?"

"Only after you answer one question. Tell me the truth,

no funny business. Would you have let me in to see Emilie if I hadn't climbed that fence?"

Gabe looked thoughtful. "I honestly don't know. I'll admit I was intrigued by you. You were exhausted, disheveled and clearly distressed. You obviously hated to be asking for help. But you had this incredible look on your face that said you weren't going to leave quietly. I wondered how far you would go to get what you wanted. When you climbed that fence, I had my answer. I knew you would never give up on anything that really mattered to you."

Gabe leaned over and kissed the tip of Cass's nose. "I was right," he said lovingly. "You didn't give up on Crudley and you didn't give up on me."

"I never will," Cass said. Then she kissed him so that neither of them would ever have any doubts again.

Epilogue

Cass fastened the delicate silver chain around her neck and contemplated her image in the mirror. Was it only the soft light reflecting from the surface of the antique locket that made her complexion seem to glow? Or was it something more? She looked and felt radiant—as if illuminated by an inner spark.

The sound of the doorbell ringing in the foyer echoed in the upstairs hallway. Cass slipped on her shoes and with a final, satisfied smile at herself in the mirror, she headed down the stairs.

A babble of voices rose from the entryway. Emilie's sweet, cheerful voice mingled with the excited squeals of Lila, Cass and Gabe's two-year-old daughter. Underlying the duet, Gabe's voice added a deep tenor counterpoint, notable for its calm in the midst of the commotion.

Gabe lifted his eyes and met Cass's gaze. After four years of marriage, that certain look of his still made her heart flutter. He smiled, and with a brief nod gestured toward Lila and Emilie, both crouched on the floor next to a picnic basket. Lila stood and began tugging on her father's sleeve. "Ask your mother, Lila," Gabe said gently but firmly.

The little girl whirled toward the staircase, her dark brown pigtails bobbing with excitement. Her determined expression indicated she was prepared to climb as many steps as necessary to find her mother. When she saw Cass was practically standing next to her, she stopped short, almost too surprised to speak. "Mama!" she finally blurted out, her chirpy voice rising higher than usual. "Look what Emma brought me!"

Emma was Lila's succinct designation for her grandma Emilie, who smiled benignly as Lila extended her arms to display the treasure she had been clutching to her chest.

"Mew," said the treasure.

Cass regarded the tiny ball of gray-and-white fur with mixed feelings. The kitten was adorable, but a new pet in the household? Cass shot Gabe an imploring look.

"Can we keep her, Mama?" Lila entreated. "Please, please, please?"

Cass nibbled reflectively on her lower lip. "I don't know, honey. Crudley is used to being the only cat in the family. He might not like having another cat living here."

"Nonsense!" Emilie asserted. "I had a long talk with him just the other day, and he seemed quite tickled with the idea."

"Emilie—" Gabe began, his inflection rising in caution.

"He wants to see her, I bet!" Lila said, clasping the kitten tightly as she ran toward the kitchen.

Emilie hurried off with her, leaving Gabe and Cass to follow. Gabe put his hand around Cass's waist and drew her close as they trailed behind. "She means well," Gabe said softly, nuzzling Cass's ears. The phrase was one they frequently had occasion to apply to Emilie.

"I know. I hope Crudley understands."

"Why should he object to having a sweet young thing around to lick his ears for him?" he asked, demonstrating.

"Stop that!" Cass demanded, her laughter undermining the order.

They paused at the kitchen door. "So far, so good," Cass said. "I don't hear any yowling, hissing or screaming."

Gabe pushed open the door to reveal a scene of perfect contentment. Crudley, roused from his usual nap in his catbed, delicately bumped noses with the kitten Lila held right up to his face. His deep, rumbling purr grew louder, then he put his head down on his paws and went back to sleep.

"He likes her," Lila announced. She released the new arrival, who blinked a few times, circled a few times, then snuggled up next to Crudley. He continued to purr.

"You see?" Emilie beamed. "I knew there would be no problem. Crudley is such an intelligent cat. He knows that in a home like this, with so much love in it, there is more than enough to go around. I dare say you could add at least a few more members to this family and still have plenty of love for everyone."

"Love for everyone," Lila echoed innocently, as Emilie flashed a knowing smile at Cass. Cass felt her cheeks begin coloring. "You two had better get a move on," Emilie continued. "You wouldn't want to be late for your own gallery showing."

"Late is fashionable," Gabe reminded her, kissing Emilie's cheek. "And artists can't be expected to adhere to the petty dictates of a clock."

"All people with good manners arrive at their own parties on time. Now scoot!"

As they drove to the gallery, Cass's thoughts kept drifting to Emilie's comments about increasing the size of her family. She had dropped several similar hints lately. Was it possible she had guessed the truth? Or was she just wishfully thinking aloud, hoping to plant an idea in Cass's head?

Gabe parked the car across the street from the gallery. "You're a million miles away. Not worried about the show, I hope? The critics and the public all love your work."

Cass shifted to lean against Gabe's shoulder. "I was thinking about what Emilie said. Sometimes I think she's been reading my mind."

"You noticed that, too, hmm?" Gabe twined his fingers through Cass's and lifted her hand to his lips. He kissed her gently. "I haven't pushed, because I know how hard you've been working to establish your career as an artist. But after the opening tonight, I don't think you'll have to worry about your future in that regard. So maybe—" He kissed her palm, and her wrist. "Maybe we can begin to concentrate on other aspects of our future."

"What other aspects do you mean?"

"Well, you always said you wanted a big family."

"I do."

"And Lila seemed delighted to have a new member in the household. Even Crudley seemed to like the idea of increasing our numbers."

"That's true."

"So I was thinking..." Gabe looked deeply into his wife's eyes. "Maybe we should get a dog, too."

Cass barely had time to register her shock before Gabe had enfolded her in his arms, laughing. He kissed her, then held her at arm's length. He shook his head in mock disappointment. "You're too easy, Mrs. Preston. In the old days, you would have found a way to wipe this smirk right off my face."

Cass folded her arms and enjoyed a smug little smile. "Oh, I have a way. I can do it with just three words. I'm already pregnant."

Her announcement had the desired effect. Gabe's stunned expression rapidly shifted through a dozen emotions before settling on something that looked to Cass's eyes like pure love.

"*You're* too easy, Mr. Preston," she whispered tenderly, stroking his cheek. "You've stopped smirking already."

"But I haven't stopped smiling—not since the day you said you'd marry me. And I know I never will."

* * * * *

twins on the doorstep

The Murdocks are back!
The adorable children from
STELLA BAGWELL'S
Twins on the Doorstep
series are all grown up and finding loves of their own. You met Emily in
THE RANCHER'S BLESSED EVENT in May 1998 and Charlie found love in
THE RANGER AND THE WIDOW WOMAN
in August 1998

Now it's Anna's turn!
Yes, the twins are about to discover true love—
and Anna's the first to lose her heart in

THE COWBOY AND THE DEBUTANTE
(SR#1334, November 1998)

And in spring of 1999 look for Adam to find the woman he can't live with—or without!

Only in Silhouette Romance.

Silhouette®

Look us up on-line at: http://www.romance.net

SRTOD2

Catch more great
HARLEQUIN™ Movies
featured on the movie channel

Premiering October 10th
Loving Evangeline
Based on the novel by *New York Times* bestselling author Linda Howard

Don't miss next month's movie!
Premiering November 14th
Broken Lullaby
Starring Mel Harris and Rob Stewart.
Based on the novel by bestselling author Laurel Pace

If you are not currently a subscriber to The Movie Channel, simply call your local cable or satellite provider for more details. Call today, and don't miss out on the romance!

the movie channel   **HARLEQUIN®**
Makes any time special ™

100% pure movies.
100% pure fun.

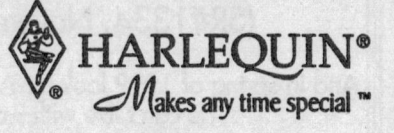

Harlequin, Joey Device, Makes any time special and Superromance are trademarks of Harlequin Enterprises Limited. The Movie Channel is a trademark of Showtime Networks, Inc., a Viacom Company.

An Alliance Television Production

PHMBPA1098

#1 *New York Times* bestselling author
NORA ROBERTS

Presents a brand-new book in the beloved MacGregor series:

THE WINNING HAND
(SSE#1202)

October 1998 in

Silhouette SPECIAL EDITION®

Innocent Darcy Wallace needs Mac Blade's protection in the high-stakes world she's entered. But who will protect Mac from the irresistible allure of this vulnerable beauty?

**Coming in March, the much-anticipated novel,
THE MACGREGOR GROOMS
Also, watch for the MacGregor stories
where it all began!**

**December 1998:
THE MACGREGORS: Serena—Caine**

**February 1999:
THE MACGREGORS: Alan—Grant**

**April 1999:
THE MACGREGORS: Daniel—Ian**

Available at your favorite retail outlet, only from

Silhouette®

Look us up on-line at: http://www.romance.net

SSEMACS1

**Coming in December 1998
from Silhouette Books...**

The BIG BAD WOLFE family is back!

WOLFE WINTER

by bestselling author

Joan Hohl

Officer Matilda Wolfe had followed in her family's law-enforcement footsteps. But the tough beauty swore she wouldn't fall in love as easily as the rest of the Wolfe pack.

Not this Christmas, not during this case...
and not with an ex-mercenary turned minister whose sexy grin haunted her dreams.

Don't miss the brand-new single-title release
WOLFE WINTER this December 1998...
only from Silhouette Books.

Available at your favorite retail outlet.

Look us up on-line at: http://www.romance.net

PSWINWOLF

Looking For More Romance?

Visit Romance.net

Look us up on-line at: http://www.romance.net

Check in daily for these and other exciting features:

Hot off the press — View all current titles, and purchase them on-line.

What do the stars have in store for you?

Horoscope

Hot deals — Exclusive offers available only at Romance.net

Plus, don't miss our interactive quizzes, contests and bonus gifts.

PWEB

Silhouette® Books

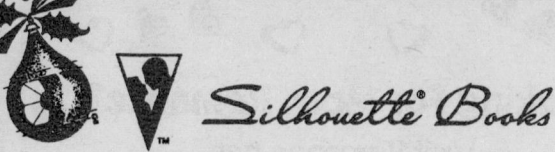

invites you to celebrate the joys
of the season December 1998 with
the Fortune Family in...

A FORTUNE'S CHILDREN CHRISTMAS

Three Fortune cousins are given exactly one year to fulfill the family traditions of wealth and power. And in the process these bachelors receive a Christmas gift more precious than mere riches from three very special women.

Don't miss this original collection of three brand-new, heartwarming stories by favorite authors:

Lisa Jackson

Barbara Boswell

Linda Turner

Look for **A FORTUNE'S CHILDREN CHRISTMAS** this December at your favorite retail outlet. And watch for more Fortune's Children titles coming to Silhouette Desire, beginning in January 1999.

Look us up on-line at: http://www.romance.net

PSFORTUNE

FOLLOW THAT BABY...

the fabulous cross-line series featuring the infamously wealthy Wentworth family...continues with:

THE DADDY AND THE BABY DOCTOR
by **Kristin Morgan**
(Romance, 11/98)

The search for the mysterious Sabrina Jensen pits a seasoned soldier—and single dad—against a tempting baby doctor who knows Sabrina's best-kept secret....

Available at your favorite retail outlet, only from

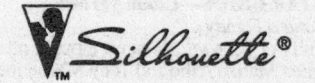

Silhouette®

Look us up on-line at: http://www.romance.net

SSEFTB2

Silhouette ROMANCE

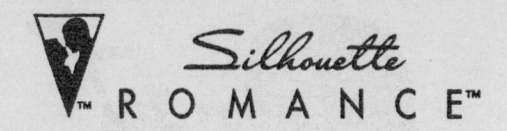

COMING NEXT MONTH

#1330 A BRIDE TO HONOR—Arlene James
Virgin Brides
Until he met dazzling beauty Cassidy Penno, Paul Spencer was prepared to make a sacrificial marriage in order to save the family's business. But now Paul was torn between family loyalty and a chance at love that could last a lifetime....

#1331 ARE YOU MY DADDY?—Leanna Wilson
Fabulous Fathers
She hated cowboys, but single mom Marty Thomas would do anything to help her son get his memory back—even pretend sexy cowboy Joe Rawlins was his father. Problem was, Joe was starting to think he might like this to be a permanent position!

#1332 PROMISES, PUMPKINS AND PRINCE CHARMING—Karen Rose Smith
Do You Take This Stranger?
Prince Charming was in disguise, and only a true Cinderella could uncover his heart! Luckily for Luke Hobart, his Cinderella was right in front of him. But Luke had to find a way to tell Becca Jacobs his true identity before the clock struck midnight and he lost his Cinderella bride forever....

#1333 THE DADDY AND THE BABY DOCTOR—Kristin Morgan
Follow That Baby!
Strapping single dad Sam Arquette needed to locate a missing person, and he hoped Amanda Lucas would help. But this baby doctor wanted nothing to do with Sam! And suddenly he was starting to wonder if finding Amanda's runaway patient would be easier than finding his way into her heart....

#1334 THE COWBOY AND THE DEBUTANTE—Stella Bagwell
Twins on the Doorstep
He was leather and chaps, she was silk and diamonds—but the attraction between Miguel Chavez and Anna Murdock Sanders defied all the rules. The ranch foreman knew better than to get involved with the boss's daughter, but soon all he wanted was to make her his—forever!

#1335 LONE STAR BRIDE—Linda Varner
Three Weddings and a Family
She wanted a family of her own. He never thought marriage was part of his future. But when Mariah Ashe and Tony Mason met, there was a sizzling attraction neither could deny. What could keep these two opposites together forever? Only love....